THE THAI WORD FOR
FORTUNE

A NOVEL BY
JULIAN MIHDI

GLASSSPIDERPUBLISHING

ISBN: 978-1-957917-16-0 (paperback edition)
ISBN: 978-1-957917-17-7 (e-book edition)

Library of Congress Control Number: 2022918985

Cover design by Judith S. Design & Creativity
www.judithsdesign.com
Published by Glass Spider Publishing
www.glassspiderpublishing.com

For Mom and my dear friend, Marc J. Cofer

Author's Note

The reader will notice that this is a bilingual text. An appendix containing all of the Thai words used in the story can be found at the back of the book, organized by chronological appearance. Footnotes are provided at the first appearance of a Thai word, but the reader is advised to refer to the appendix if that Thai word is repeated later in the text. Additionally, it should be noted that I have, in some cases, opted for contextual translations rather than academic ones. These are in cases where a literal translation would fall short of conveying what is actually being expressed by the Thai speaker.

CHAPTER ONE

It wasn't long after my mother passed that my girlfriend started winning the Thai lottery. As I saw it, the chance that they weren't connected was very small.

Let me add that there's no way to politely verbalize that in conversation, and I know it. That's probably why I didn't see many people in Chiang Mai after the funeral. On my flight back over the Pacific, I mindlessly crunched on stale pretzels and washed them down with ginger ale, hardly knowing where I was. I could still smell the odor of wet soil at my mother's grave on the hillside and still feel the mushiness of the earth under my black dress shoes. You know what they say about April showers. Truth be told, the rose I placed on her casket felt heavier than the casket itself. Pallbearers' perceptions aren't the most empirical, however.

I had a friend once who came from a long line of morticians. His irreverence knew no bounds, and I loved him for it. He chain-smoked, cursed his luck, and howled with laughter when I marveled at his prolific record with women. He told me he liked me because I was the "goodie-two-shoes version" of himself.

"Jesus, Prism, how are you so damn positive?" he'd say in his Carolina drawl.

As a rapper, you never want to hear someone call you a goodie-two-shoes. But guys like that are honest because life is a harlot and they only know extremes. That's why people trust them to know if it will rain at their mother's funeral.

Of course, he was right about me. I'm a hopelessly positive guy. I remember reading that Camus novel where the guy goes to his mother's wake, basically shrugs it off, then kills someone he doesn't know on a beach. I'm not cynical enough to be that psycho. (I was still young enough to pronounce "Camus" like it rhymed with "campus.") My fatal flaw as a cynic is seeing meaning where there should only be emptiness. That's the problem with most American Buddhists, in fact. I'm not really a Buddhist, but becoming an orphan would have been harder if I didn't have *something*.

My Carolina mourning shuddered to a close. I bade my teary farewells, caught a plane to Hong Kong, and before I knew it I was climbing back onto my motorbike in Chiang Mai. No matter what changes in your life, this city will never deceive you. It has the haunting quality of remaining more or less exactly how you remember it. Old-timers will be quick to remind me that only thirty years ago, everything was still dirt roads and tall grass. Imperceptibly, the dirt roads became paved, yes, and shopping malls were pulled out of some Singaporean's pocketbook, yet none of that succeeded in altering Chiang Mai's personality. International capital, financial investment—these things must contort themselves into sundry yoga positions to survive the city's nonchalance.

Not that I know anything about that stuff. I only stay here because this place doesn't punish me for being right-brained, as the rest of the world seems so intent on doing. For example, a date is considered a success if both parties mutually succeed in meeting. If one hangs around more than ten minutes waiting for the other, the label *soul mate* is not out of the question. Marriage is an ever-present danger, especially when one takes into account the visa benefits such an agreement entails. The spontaneity of Thai culture, however, generally makes for more fluid relationships. Every commitment bears the asterisk of likely avoidance—this is true across society, from the trivial level of friend circles right up to government offices.

It drives some *farangs*[1] crazy; others plan their life around not ever having to make plans.

Somehow, in the Himalayan malaise of hot mornings and aborted work plans, I met a young woman who spoke English and took life semi-seriously. I drank an iced Americano and downed thick slices of *sapparot*[2] as she outlined the general shape of her story, sometimes obtusely. (Some Thai dates give you the feeling of being the blind man in the proverb of the elephant, fumbling by fits and starts to understand who you're confronting.)

Her name was Nim. Many of her essential details I'd only come to understand later.

Nim struck me as the kind of woman whose movements happen in a blur. She was the picture of the optimistic entrepreneur, friendly and sharp of mind, more often than not occupied with a brief phone call that, nevertheless, always seemed to carry great import. Her fashion sense was bold and made the rest of the café appear black and white in comparison.

My first impression was that she was intensely interesting, if only from a material perspective. Nim's dark hair hung to her shoulders, and she wore a mustard-yellow blouse with puffy shoulders that daringly bared her midriff. In short, there was nothing supernatural about her, nor did there need to be. Hers was a light presence. That was enough.

---

[1] *Farang(s)*: Foreigner (ฝรั่ง)

[2] *Sapparot*: Pineapple (สับปะรด)

We met for coffee again. Then she invited me over for dinner at her condo near the university. "I never have been the good cook, na," she laughed, cooing in sympathy with herself.

I confirmed her statement on multiple occasions, though her vegan passionfruit cakes started to show glimmers of promise. Nim was a worldly, cosmopolitan girl whose brain buzzed with numbers, charts, business plans—cooking was a superfluous skill, as was driving herself around town. With her reliance on instant Grab rides, she may as well have had a personal chauffeur. Nim lived like a princess in a city with an ancient history of princesses—hardly the typical profile of someone destined to hit it big in the lottery.

After several evenings of anime-and-chill, neither of us had developed any objections to being intimate, and we naturally became lovers. Nim's English and my Thai—somewhat suspect articles on their own—found the perfect complement in one another. Our conversations were like catalogs of missing vocabulary: one sentence might innocently feature three language transitions. Our pillow talk would be nearly unintelligible to all but a few unlucky observers. Then, inevitably, a notification would sound from her bag, and she was back to juggling phones, sometimes meeting my gaze with a slyly arched eyebrow.

Her condo was situated in the Nimman district on the west side, a tangle of little avenues called *sois*[3] with steaming shabu diners and the overpriced Thai merchandise that Chinese tourists seem to love. Many of us suspect that they teleport from Beijing into the basement of the nearby Maya shopping center and gradually fan out from there, such is the volume of their numbers in this area.

We often hung out at my apartment. "Look like this area can

---

[3] *Sois*: Avenues (ซอย)

hear the birds," Nim would say in the morning, sighing with delight.

For all her mathematical know-how, she was quite sentimental. And she was right. I lived in a Shangri-La of serenity at the foot of the mountain known as Doi Suthep, among the most sacred in the kingdom. My vine-covered balcony floated in a sea of treetops and temple spires, admitting a direct view of the mountain. Bird chatter filled the air and, on cool mornings, the temple atop Doi Suthep was wreathed in low-skimming clouds. The sound of the monastery gong reached my open window before daybreak. Thai monks clad in orange moved noiselessly through the streets for alms. The dogs would go crazy; I was rarely awake to notice.

By now, one may observe that I am not a standard office-goer and, owing to my earlier discussion of "plans," that I even hold a certain disregard for involuntary schedules. There are spies around Chiang Mai that would probably give you a similar line. While some of our choices of outdoor cafés may align, I can't claim to be that sophisticated—I can barely unlock my smartphone some days. Nor can I be described as a person of wealth, lapping from the breast milk of privilege and private accounts.

It is enough to say that I get along by strategically using my laptop in laid-back environments, as do many other twentysomethings in this town. It is no great feat, and I would be at great pains to elaborate on it any more than I have. What is this talk of "work," anyway, but a stealthy way of dropping someone's pin on the social terrain as a means to generate conversations that only become increasingly contrived? Think of me as a Wi-Fi warrior, if that helps.

And a white rapper, for that matter. Not of the nut-grabbin' variety, mind you; I'm not out here like Michael Rapaport on IG, making brash statements and starting every sentence with three *yo's*. I'm just a poet who lost patience with the written word.

The thing is, white rappers always have to introduce themselves with qualifications. None of us want to be mistaken for the stereotype. We're kind of like UFO abductees. People look at you weird, and no one really takes you seriously, but that's mainly outside of hip-hop. The culture accepts you if you bring originality. My fascination is with words, how you can isolate syllables of one word to fit them together with the syllables of another word in rhyme, like bodies intertwined in a multitude of Kama Sutra positions.

I go by the name of Prism. My ex gave me that name because my lyrics, according to her, "capture the clusterfuck of human life in all its flashing colors." She probably changed her opinion soon after, but the name stuck.

My friends and I perform our songs around the city from time to time. Nothing crazy; we usually end up on the mic at places where Dutch guys take their girlfriends to hear electronic music and get cheap drugs. Sometimes, they stick around. We get style points with stragglers who commend us for being exemplars of "the real hip-hop sound."

One time, I brought Nim with me to a performance. She was dressed in one of her eye-popping blouses that made everything go fuzzy around her. When I looked over, I saw she was attempting to nod her head with a somewhat vacant expression. The next time I looked, she was talking in a short burst of urgency on her phone, her face turned away.

"*Geng mak mak*[4]!" was Nim's simple, congratulatory note after the show. Perhaps that's all one needs to hear from his girlfriend.

The first time Nim told me about winning the lottery, in fact, I was in the studio with my favorite Thai producer, who makes

---

[4] *Geng mak mak*: "Great job!" (เก่งมาก ๆ)

music under the moniker of Unknown. (This makes him the source of all inspirational quotes online, he tells me.) We were preparing a mic-check when I saw Nim's face buzz across my phone screen.

"Prism, Prism," her voice gushed in enthusiasm. "Right now, I have the crazy thing to tell you, na! Where are you?"

I told her.

"Okay," she said, "I will tell you when we meet. Today my friend *len huay*[5] with my numbers, and it looks *so* lucky. It all happened from your house, na."

"From my house, what do you mean?"

I heard her chuckle in triumph at my confusion. "Yes, I will tell you at dinner, *na khá*[6]."

My ignorance of lotteries was impressively total. I knew nothing of how they worked—not in the Thai Kingdom, not in the States, not anywhere. I was raised to believe gambling was a sin and, as I already had my pet vices, thought nothing of avoiding it altogether. The only lottery I had any familiarity with was a fictional one: Borges' *Lottery in Babylon*, which I had found in a book named *Labyrinths* collecting dust atop my Wi-Fi router. In this lottery, winning money was only one potential outcome. One could also select a ticket that sentenced him to death, or worse. Everything was left to chance; it was possible that every event transpiring in that Babylon was the outcome of a random drawing. Not exactly the Powerball, is it? Short of these *ficciones*, I only knew that Thais took on the lotto numbers with legendary zeal, incorporating every superstition imaginable—but that will come later.

I met up with Nim at a quaint eatery named Mindful Eating, right next to a temple known as Wat Pong Noi close to my

---

[5] *Len huay*: "Played the lottery." (เล่นหวย)

[6] *Na kha*: An expression of female politeness (คะ)

apartment. Around dinnertime, the air was always thick with smoke rolling off the grills as food vendors lined the street at the old forest temple's gates. The eatery was nestled in a cut-through *soi* in such a way that it was easy to miss. There was no building, only a gated green space, white tents, tables, and chairs. In the back stood a luminous shanty fashioned into a cocktail bar. The cuisine was very un-Thai, featuring exquisite gyros with green pesto and hummus, and the owner looked to be of Mediterranean origin.

Tonight, Nim was decked out in a zebra-print collared shirt and blouse whose neckline beckoned my gaze. Bracelets twinkled from her wrists.

"So what's all this about the lottery?" I asked, having cleared the hurdle of small talk.

"Ahhh! Prism, I think you will not believe this, but it happened *in the real…*"

The waitress arrived with our smoothies in tall, clear glasses—red for her, yellow for me. Young Thai women are so obsessed with taking pictures of fresh-served menu items that you'd think all of them had been enlisted as influencers. Nim was no exception. She giggled at my long-suffering look, patting my hand in apology.

"And so?"

"Okay," she began, puckering her lips on the straw, "you remember that I stay at your place a couple nights ago, *chai mai*[7]?"

I affirmed.

"Yes, and in the morning I go to *hong nam*[8], and did you know that something happened to me there?"

I raised my eyebrows and gave her a look.

"Prism!"

---

[7] *Chai mai*: "Right?" (ใช่ไหม)

[8] *Hong nam*: Bathroom (ห้องน้ำ)

"Okay, okay, so you're in the bathroom…"

"*Chai*[9], and I'm washing my face, and you know? I hear the voice, it was talking to me. It sounded like a man's voice, na. He say, 'How much money you have now?' and…" Nim broke off at the severity of my expression.

"You heard a man's voice?"

She nodded.

"And this wasn't your phone or anything like that?"

"*Mai chai*[10], my phone was on the bed, still charging! So I hear him say that, right? I told him I only have 2,000 *baht*[11]. It was so crazy. He told me to buy the lottery ticket and use the number 96. My thinking looked like, 'Huh?' Because I never play the Thai lottery before…"

I repeated what she said back to me, prone to misinterpretation as I was. She nodded and laughed in agreement. I raised my eyebrows and took a deep sip of frozen mango. My brain began fragmenting into ice-cold shards of sunshine; I winced at the pain and rubbed my temples.

"So how much did you win?"

"Huh?"

"I said—"

"No, you remember what I tell you on the phone?"

Our chicken gyros arrived, and we lapsed into carnivorous silence. This lady's tzatziki sauce was an authentic work of art. Warm pita bread slathered in the medley of yogurt, cucumber, and lemon is better than ice cream to me, especially in Chiang Mai where the *yang* of Thai food is law. Nim took a napkin and wiped the corner

---

[9] *Chai*: "Yes" (ใช่)

[10] *Mai chai*: "No" (ไม่ใช่)

[11] *Baht*: Thai unit of currency, 30=1 USD at the time of writing (บาท)

of my mouth, tittering in disapproval.

"What did you tell me on the phone?"

"I call my friend and tell her the numbers, *chai maï*, and you know what happened?"

"She won?"

"20,000 *baht*, na!"

"Seriously? Why didn't you buy any tickets yourself?"

Nim placed an index finger on her chin. "Hmm, when it happened, I think it's only my imagining. I just wake up, still sleepy, you know?"

"But you really heard the voice, it wasn't just in your head, right?"

"*Chaï*, it was like someone speaking to me, but I couldn't see them."

I shook my head and started rolling a cigarette. Psychic girlfriends, strangely enough, weren't in themselves a novelty in my life. But usually, you can *sense* that sort of thing. Sometimes, women like that are more introverted, withdrawn, somewhat aloof at parties. Or maybe their sixth sense reveals itself in their bedroom decor: Tibetan prayer flags, Ganesha altars, that sort of thing. You know that they see and feel things that you can't, and that's just the way it is.

Nim wasn't like that. She lived, as far as I could tell, on the surface of life. There were no hidden rooms with her. She had K-pop tabs open as soon as she woke up, for Christ's sake. That was the most amazing thing to me, really. A person of Nim's naivete would normally be shaken by such an experience. Instead, she was merely lighthearted about the whole thing, if not downright amused.

"So there's a polite ghost at my apartment who wants to help you win the lottery?" I asked, exhaling a cloud of tobacco.

"You have to make friends with him, na," Nim laughed, picking up her phone.

"He never said anything to *me* before," I protested.

"He's a Thai person, maybe he's shy about the *farang¹*."

"Oh, God," I grinned. "So people die and there's still a language barrier?"

"I dunno," Nim said, carelessly tossing her head. *"Check bin¹²
kha!"*

I had a steady head nod going to the restaurant's playlist. DJ Quik's "Do I Love Her" was thumping on the speakers, and I felt my mood shift. I'm from the East Coast, and even I know Quik is rap's greatest producer. He's California's bodhisattva of P-funk. The replay value is off the charts. That was the first time I'd heard a Quik track played at a Thai establishment, kind of like finding a four-leaf clover in a snow drift. Normally, the best American music we get in Chiang Mai is the bluegrass twang of "Country Road." Five-year-olds will literally belt out the chorus. I'll never understand how Thai rock bands got stuck on our oldies stations.

We were walking back to my motorbike, the chorus of "Do I Love Her" spinning in my head. I was driving this old Yamaha Nouvo my friend gave me, blue and temperamental. Wat Pong Noi was shrouded in moonlit silence, most of the vendors having gone home. I looked at Nim's downturned face in the glow of the streetlamps. *Maybe there's more to her than meets the eye,* I thought.

"I think the Night Safari is still open 'til 10 p.m.," I teased, tugging the sleeve of her zebra-stripe blouse.

"Prism! *Mai wai luy¹³*"

She climbed onto the motorbike behind me, resting her hand

---

¹² *Check bin*: Common phrase for settling a bill (เช็คบิล)

¹³ *Mai wai luy:* "I just *can't* with you!" (ไม่ไหวเลย)

on my shoulder. My apartment was less than five minutes away. I savored the brisk mountain air as we lazily rounded the curves in the road. My eyes were always attracted this time of year by the roadside cables hung with Chinese lanterns—red, yellow, orange, blue. I thought about how I'd start my next journal entry: *Nim was at my apartment when she met a friendly ghost specializing in lottery numbers…*

It would be the first of many entries.

CHAPTER TWO

The lottery is the official religion of the Thai Kingdom, with Buddhism a close second. Some might even say the lottery is the reason for the Buddha's popularity. He operates through a sophisticated network of spirit shrines and carefully placed pagodas, all of which function to exact binding promises from Thai citizens in exchange for the currency of earthly fortune. The monks are his ever-loyal agents—from their lips issue oaths, incantations, holy numbers. People line up at their temples to do business with the fortune lenders. Meditation, which I'm told was once the centerpiece of the Eightfold Path, is little more than a hasty formality followed by group photos.

Wikipedia calls it superstition; I call it the economy of karma. It's not for me to judge whether it's right or wrong. I'll leave it to other *farangs* to make that commentary, as is their specialty. If a prosperous life merely costs some monthly donations to a temple, a few selfless acts, what's the harm? I can easily think of other religious institutions that have done worse. The Thai lottery, you might say, has the purpose of normalizing the more mysterious currents of life.

It works like this. You buy a ticket, maybe around eighty *baht*.

There's a six-digit number. If all six match, you win, perhaps, a million dollars. You can win smaller sums with five matching numbers, four, and so on. Lottery days are the first and sixteenth of every month—come rain, hell, or apocalypse. You can buy these tickets anytime, anywhere. Just look for the lone woman under the parasol, at a market, at a temple. The whole separation-of-church-and-gambling thing never went through out here. Such thinking doesn't make it in this part of the world.

After Nim won money in the lottery a second time, it seemed to confirm that my apartment was the main factor. Since her first experience, I'd made a point of burning sage every morning before I made coffee. It's hard to say whether this achieved anything besides reducing the odor of my dirty laundry. Life had continued as normal, really. I always walked out onto my street at 8:30 a.m. to buy papayas and mangos, then I would come back and try not to cut my fingers as I peeled them over the sink. The little house geckos squirted across my walls with haste. Their instincts allowed them nothing but terror in the presence of humans.

It was a Saturday. The sound of traditional Thai music floated from the *muban*[14] loudspeakers like the voice of a mountain goddess wafting over the cafés and alleyways. They usually played this music on the weekends. On sunny afternoons you felt yourself falling under its trance, leaning back on your chair with a yawn.

My friend Gabe was dropping by for a visit on his way home. Gabe was an older gentleman from Oregon enjoying his Chiang Mai retirement in stubborn solitude. "It doesn't get any worse," he said to me once, "than finding yourself in the company of expats." He was a kind man under his gloomy exterior.

I'd met him by chance up on the Samoeng Loop, a meandering

---

[14] *Muban:* Village/neighborhood (หมู่บ้าน)

route through the mountains where it wasn't uncommon to see mahouts riding their elephants on the road's shoulder. I took a spill on my motorbike one day up there and it happened to be in front of his house. He helped clean me up and gave me some bandages. Afterward, Gabe invited me to stay for coffee and a smoke.

The green-covered slopes filled my eyes as he described his former life as a cop and, later, a "street pharmacist." He befriended the junkies, alienated his fellow cops, and smoked "doobies" on the beat like a badass. Gabe's demeanor was quiet, steady, no-nonsense. His bald head was pale and he always seemed to be wearing shades.

It was easy for me to coax stories out of him, stories which often had considerable shock value, but Gabe recited them flatly, without relish. His Thai was woeful and he knew it. Sometimes I helped translate for him when he had a misunderstanding with his landlady. He wasn't the sort of guy who stood on ceremony, that much was clear.

I was rolling up a cigarette when someone else showed up at my door. It was my hippie Thai friend, Hop.

"Prism, *yo, yo*," he greeted me, poking the air with pointed fingers like a rapper. He always did that when he saw me.

I later realized that I was probably the only person with whom he could perform such affectations. We had a mutual friend (a more serious sort of guy) who had taken a teaching job out in Mae On. Hop had shoulder-length hair, a sweet, open sort of face, and always wore frumpled clothes. Allegedly a "handyman," he had never, to our knowledge, held any one job for more than a month. He often showed up at my apartment uninvited, and usually left just as suddenly.

"Yeah, let's smoke together and hear this, man," Hop announced, waving a Bob Marley record in his hand. "We don't need the government, only love...peace...and *beautiful ladies*," he added, cackling crassly.

Our pacifist, I could see, was already intoxicated, reeking of beer and marijuana. Hop's eyes were bloodshot. His movements were like that of a soccer player who isn't sure if he's exiting the match or staying on the field. He smiled mildly as I gestured toward the old record player next to my bookcase. I watched as he fumbled with the sleeve, turned it around, probed, then finally extracted the vinyl, his own sword from the stone.

"*Puh-un maa laew*[15] *krub*[16]," I informed Hop as Gabe started backing his car into my driveway. (That was one of Gabe's old habits from his time in the streets. "Always be prepared to haul ass as fast as you can," he counseled me once.)

Hop only nodded inattentively, absorbed in his imperative to spread the light of Bob Marley through our immediate reality. That was around the time I invited Nim over with a quick text message. I had no idea it was the fifteenth of the month—the eve of the new lottery. I was more concerned with making the effort to include her in more of my impromptu social gatherings, and I was also aware that it had been over a week since we last met. That was all.

Cane in hand, the ex-cop pulled himself out of his black Prius with a curt nod. "Tell ya what, if I had known about all those damn protests, I wouldn't have come to the city at all..."

"Yeah, I heard it was a mess around Tha Pae Gate," I sympathized, shaking his hand. "Gabe, this is my buddy, Hop."

The latter was by now sitting cross-legged on the floor next to the record player, a joint smoldering between his fingers. Hop

---

[15] *Puh-un maa laew:* "My friend is here." (เพื่อนมาแล้ว)

[16] *Krub:* An expression of male politeness (ครับ)

greeted the elder with a *wai*[17] and two soft hellos.

"He's got the right idea," Gabe quipped, nodding his head in recognition. He emitted several grunts and plopped down on my sofa. "God forbid I say anything about what these people do in their own country, but it's a goddamned nuisance when you have kids camped out on a crosswalk, traffic's at a standstill...I don't see social progress, I see a traffic jam from hell."

"There was a big event on the university campus last night, too," I offered, "looked to be around a thousand students out there holding signs."

Hop offered his joint to me, but I shook my head and pointed in Gabe's direction. Weed only succeeds in making me lose track of what I've said and second-guess actions I've yet to take.

"Well," Gabe began, leaning over to pluck the joint from Hop's fingers, "they say it's a big student protest, this big grassroots thing like we had in the '70s. I call bullshit. That stuff doesn't happen anymore. Everything is corporate now. It's probably just a political campaign for this guy, uh—"

"Thanathorn?"

"Whomever," Gabe said, waving his hand and taking a long drag. "I keep my nose out of politics. It's the same as back home. Too many wolves in sheep's clothing. Now they've got the kids charged up about a revolution, and you know what? When they get out of school, they'll likely be the ones paying for it..."

Hop, meanwhile, had surrendered himself to Bob Marley's persuasions. The Wailers' opening horns on "Revolution" stabbed the air; he swayed back and forth like one in hypnosis, a serene smile on his face. "*Revolution...Revolution*," the hippie mumbled sweetly under his breath, oblivious to Gabe's remarks. He suddenly turned

---

[17] *Wai*: A universal sign of respect (ไหว้)

and regarded me with a glazed expression.

"Prism, you have to understand...there is such a pure feeling, in love, in the protest, when my people stand up to the government, you see?"

Hop, overwhelmed at the thought, shook his head and made a mournful sound in his throat. He raised his hand to summon another sentence.

"How can they not know that love is the only way *to know*...?"

Hop appeared to have more to say, but his thoughts were derailed by the part where the backup singers sing about lightning and thunder. He closed his eyes in ecstasy like a student on the hills of Woodstock.

I glanced back at Gabe, who was staring out the screen door with a grave look. How could I bridge the gap? My eye fell on the copy of *Labyrinth*s atop the Wi-Fi router. Blowing the dust off the cover, I picked the book up and offered it to Gabe.

"Ever read any of this?"

He took it from me but barely gave it a glance. "I remember when I was still in the force," Gabe said in his gravelly voice, "I used to take in this prostitute. Heroin junkie, Nicaraguan gal. She would come to my place just to get off the streets for a while. She was so thin, there was barely any of her left. Skin and bones. She told me she was a daughter of one of those Contra rebels, you know? He deserted her when she was 11, left her to the streets, not even a thought.

"Bought groceries, and she'd go through everything in a night. Eggs, yogurt, pancakes, cereal—everything. After about two weeks, the color would be back in her face, and then the cycle would begin again. Wake up one morning and she's gone. Some of my cash would be missing too, hell..." Gabe cast his eyes on the cross-legged Hop, lost in reggae space. "That's what all that revolution stuff really gets people. Broken homes and heroin addicts. Ah, she was a pretty thing," he added to himself sadly.

"Wow," I said, suppressing a laugh. Gabe's stories always reminded me of something out of *The Wire*.

Just then, Nim came in through the front door. She was wearing a black jumpsuit that showed some leg, along with a yellow handbag hanging from her shoulder that said *Be Kind To Foreigner* in black lettering. Nim coughed a couple of times, waving a hand in front of her face and giving me a look. The room was by now hazy with smoke.

"Hop! *Mao ri-yung[18], kha?*"

"*Mai tung, mai tung[19],*" Hop replied good-naturedly.

"Hello!" Nim said, turning to Gabe.

"How ya doin'?"

"This is my friend Gabe," I informed Nim.

"*Kha,*" she said politely, lowering her head as she stepped past the old man to sit down.

Gabe pointed at the words on her yellow handbag. "Don't forget, now," he chuckled with a wink.

Nim looked at me questioningly.

"Be kind to foreigner, *chai mai?*"

"Ahh yes, the new bag from my friend."

Soon enough, Hop, overflowing with revolutionary spirit, rose and told me that he would be back soon. That was the last we saw of him for the night. Nim intuited this about ten minutes after he left and told me as much. His Bob Marley record remained untouched, the cover and sleeve still on the floor. By now it was dark and the cicadas had started their drunken chorus. Gabe lingered

---

[18] *Mao ri-yung:* "Are you drunk yet?" (เมาหรือยัง)
[19] *Mai tung:* "Not quite." (ไม่ถึง)

for another forty minutes before announcing his departure.

"She's a keeper," he told me as I saw him out to his Prius. "That other kid's a nutcase, though."

The next day, Nim's friends were clamoring to talk with me. Nim had pulled down 120,000 *baht* at the lottery and they wanted to know what, exactly, had made me invite her over to my place at the last minute.

"I dunno," I said, "I thought she might enjoy hanging out with my oddball friends."

That, and that alone, apparently, had been the magic key. After the guys had left and we went to bed, Nim had a dream. A man appeared—she understood him to be the same person whose voice she heard in my bathroom. He conversed with her in the manner of a well-bred mentor. "I think he is *khon dee*[20]," Nim told me. After a brief interview, the man provided her with the lucky numbers and wished her luck. When I asked Nim what he looked like, she only shook her head.

"I couldn't see his face, it looked like...sorry, how to say in English?" Nim was waving her hand back and forth in front of her face.

"You mean, like, a blur?"

"*Chai*! It looked impossible to see his face. *Arrai wa*[21]...?"

"So an anonymous donor," I said aloud to myself. "And how did he give you the numbers?"

"He just spoke them to me, and then I wake up, type it into my phone, and back to sleep. You know, Prism, it looks so crazy, it's my first time playing the Thai lottery—and I win 120,000 *baht*. What?!"

---

[20] *Khon dee:* A good person (คนดี)

[21] *Arrai wa:* "What the hell?" (อะไรว้า)

I did some quick calculations. "I mean yeah, someone in the spirit world just helped you win four thousand dollars, it's insane—so you think this guy is living here in my apartment?"

"Now it's two times," Nim reasoned, "and both times at your apartment. I think you have the lucky ghost living with you na, Prism…"

I shook my head. It was the perfect Thai yarn of ghosts, luck, money, and romance, all coming together like the script for a serialized TV drama. It drew a grin to reflect on the bizarre scene of Hop's *Dazed and Confused* act paired with Gabe's dark narratives of rigged politics and famished hookers. Somehow the combination was auspicious—enough, at least, to serve as a pretext for Nim's appearance, which had inexplicably led to pure cash money from an invisible Samaritan.

There wasn't room for two ghosts at my apartment, though. I knew my mother's was already there. Her presence pervaded dream after dream like the shadow of a fragrance; my mornings were a postscript of her visits. In dying, she hadn't completely departed. She likely wanted to monitor my hygiene from an angelic realm, I guessed.

I feel self-conscious in putting these words to paper…normally I would never talk about this. After all, am I supposed to? Or is this not a secret we agree to withhold in world society? We permit the vague sentimentality of "she's always with you" but forbid anyone to mention that seeing disincarnated family members is more common than *never*.

It was the tail end of the rainy season in Chiang Mai, early September. The skies and the scattered orchids carry on a torrid love affair while the rest of us stand by and deal with the consequences. Brief rainfalls in the mid-afternoon send motorists under the nearest awning, filling cratered *sois* with puddles that can swallow a whole wheel. There's usually a ten-minute lull in traffic, the skies clear, and the drone of engines once again fills the void.

Some cities grow outward. Chiang Mai, bound by the river to its east and mountains on all sides, grows ever inward. Scornful of skyscrapers, it finds its modern spirit by multiplying the lines of travel that connect one point to the other within its boundaries. If you find yourself in the ancient center, surrounded by the walls of the moat, you'll likely become lost in twisting alleyways that make the square seem bigger than it is. (Each of which holds the possibility of a bohemian oasis that only appears if you're searching for something else.) Gnarled trees serve as primary points of reference, but they've become indifferent gatekeepers in the post-iPhone age.

Several days after Nim's big win, I happened to be hanging out on the south side of the moat. I'd just eaten a spicy bowl of *khao soi*[22] with a drumstick of chicken and pickled vegetables floating in the broth. Three dollops of chili pepper left me coughing up a storm. I rolled a cigarette and stepped outside to smoke.

Supposedly called to a studio session by a producer friend, I was awaiting the inevitable call of cancellation. He goes by the name of Open Source (a play on the name of an old nineties crew). It's not that he's a bad guy. Source just seems stuck in a loop of boosting expectations to an impossible level before terminating the follow-through.

Other friends have had similar experiences. The thing is, some of his music is awesome. There's no question Source is a talented guy, and I'm always down with the *idea* of doing projects with him, but it's painful to see the same idea slowly bleed out like a grounded dove as days turn to months.

He comes from a Cuban family in New Jersey—really nice guy.

---

[22] *Khao soi*: Coconut-based soup with egg noodles (ข้าวซอย)

When you see him at a party, Source is the picture of finesse. He always puts his hand on my shoulder and ushers me outside to talk in private. For some reason, I always get drawn in by his new visions. Then the death cycle of rescheduling begins.

The phone call came, but it wasn't from Open Source. It was an "unauthorized" number. I usually ignore those calls because they weird me out. Somehow, I felt compelled to answer this one. It sounded like one of those automated voices you get from a service provider—at first. Quickly, I realized this was something totally different. There was a metallic voice addressing me by my government name.

"Hello? Who is this?"

"The afternoon is pleasant. Come to the Chiang Mai Center Library to receive instructions."

"Instructions? Wha—"

I tried speaking some Thai but the line was already dead. The name rang a bell. I looked up the Chiang Mai Center Library on my phone. *I remember this place,* I said to myself. It was officially known as the *École française d'Extrême Orient.* Sometimes they had events there of an academic nature; I had gone with a friend once to hear an author talk about Christian missionaries and colonialism in the Thai Kingdom.

I must've left my number on a sign-in sheet, I thought.

Maybe it was some kind of freaky promotional thing they were doing. I looked at my phone again; I was loath to spend any more time watching the fountains in the moat's canal, waiting for Open Source to hit me back.

I flicked the cigarette butt into a sunlit patch of the gutter. Screw it, why not? The part about instructions still confused me, but I was feeling adventurous.

I jumped on my Yamaha, finally got it to start, and merged into the afternoon traffic. The library was situated near the river, east of the square. They evidently knew how to bait their clients with cliffhangers.

CHAPTER THREE

The library sat in a gated property of lavish palm trees. I drove my bike up the gravel pathway and parked it off to the side of the entrance. The lot was empty, but through the glass windows I could see a figure seated at the welcome desk. Two French flags hung limply from their staffs above the front door. It was a modest wood-frame building, made in the classic Lanna style, with open balconies on either side shaded in the greenery. I stepped inside.

The lady at the desk didn't look up, which was sort of strange. I walked through the foyer into another room filled with books, all in French. They were set on wood shelves attached to metal frames. Everything was quiet. I idly picked up a book—*Élise ou la Vraie Vie* by Claire Etcherelli. I can't speak a lick besides *"oui, oui."* I've always dreamed of a French girlfriend who could make me trilingual, but the closest I've gotten is a Spanish flame who only reminded me how poor my conjugations were.

I heard someone behind me say my government name. I whirled around. It was the lady from the desk. *"Sawadee kha[23],"* she

---

[23] *Sawadee kha:* Standard Thai greeting (สวัสดี)

said, pressing her hands together in a *wai*, bowing deeply. I returned the greeting and she led me back to the front room.

The first thing I noticed was that she was dressed in the impeccably traditional Lanna style: a long-sleeved white shirt tucked into a purple skirt that reached all the way to her feet. It wasn't uncommon to see women dress in the traditional manner from time to time; some professionals do so on Fridays, or national holidays. This particular day was neither. Sitting down, I began to ask the woman how she knew who I was, but I found myself cut off.

"*An nang-suh ru-yang kha*[24]?" she queried crisply, pushing a big book across the desk and clasping her hands.

Stunned, I looked at the book, then back at the lady in front of me. She looked to be in her forties. Her hair was pulled back into a bun, and her stare was unwavering. I felt slightly unnerved. Thai people almost never speak to a fluent foreigner so brusquely.

At that point, I happened to notice something on the wall behind her head. It was a calendar with a black-and-white picture of the old king—Rama IX, not his son. That in itself wasn't so peculiar, given his popularity. I looked further down. According to the calendar, it was February...February of *1983*.

The librarian pried the heavy book open. It didn't smell like any other book I'd come across. Old books usually smell friendly, maybe because their appreciation for being read increases with age. This one was different. It had a pungent scent that made me lean back.

"*Ah, du dee na kha*[25]," the librarian urged me.

There was something mechanical about how she spoke. I forced myself to lean forward, then took a sharp breath. The lines

---

[24] *An nang-suh ru-yang kha:* "Have you read this book yet?" (อ่านหนังสือหรือยัง)
[25] *Ah, du dee na kha:* "Have a good look." (ดูดี)

34

of text were undulating, like the streamers attached to the back of jet planes.

I shook my head, closed my eyes, opened them again. Nothing changed. The pages rippled like the surface of a pond. I squinted my eyes, trying to focus. The only thing I could make out was the Thai name *Naresuan*.

A high-pitched whistling sound pierced the air. I grabbed my ears and bent my head down. Two hands pressed firmly on my shoulders and I jumped with a start. I found myself staring at a tall French-looking woman with long, curly hair, watching me with an amazed expression. I looked back in the Thai librarian's direction, but she was gone. So was the book. In its place was a MacBook computer that *definitely* hadn't been there before. My eyes widened, and I looked back at the new woman in front of me, fumbling for an explanation as I stood up.

"Who you speak to?" she asked in a thick accent.

"Your Thai employee, who is she? She was just…" I trailed off as I saw her expression.

"No Thai employee today, I am the only one here."

"But you didn't see…she had a purple skirt on, with a big book…"

She shook her head preemptively, starting to back away. "You are mistaken, *monsieur*, you are mistaken…!"

At this point I was more than freaked out. I turned on my heels and beat it out of there. I got to my motorbike and slumped onto the seat, heart pounding. *What in the holy hell just happened to me?*

Looking at my phone gave me another surprise. When I arrived at the library, it was around 3:15. I hadn't been in there for more than twenty minutes, tops. Somehow it was now 5:30 in the evening—a full two hours later.

My phone was flooded with notifications. Open Source's text

was the first I saw: *Got caught up 2day, will have studio time nxt week.* No surprise there. Hop had sent me one of his classic *Hey man* texts that usually meant he was passing through my *muban*. Nim was asking me to dinner and seemed flustered about some business interaction. I sighed and began to start my bike, giving the library one last look. Maybe it was time to quit smoking, I thought to myself.

For some reason, the music app on my phone started playing a DJ Quik song. It felt weird, but I let it play. My keys already in the ignition, I let my hand rest on the throttle for a moment.

The French flags flapped in exotic ease, as they had before, and everything stood silent in the setting sun's penumbra of gold. I felt like I was in one of those movies where they contrast scenes of desolation and carnage with a Louie Armstrong tune. There I was, freshly spit out of some vibrational tornado, listening to Quik flip porno-style rhymes on "Somethin' 4 Tha Mood." Exhaling, I finally turned the keys and watched the odometer light up. *Pai laew!*[26]

Hightailing it through the gates of the French library, I headed over to Nim's place. I certainly wasn't "in the mood" for anything besides staying in and laying low. I still had chills going up my spine, spreading across my skin with a tingly feeling.

A snake of taillights crept around the corners of the square. I tried diverting myself with more thoughts about Compton's finest, DJ Quik. Growing up where I did, none of us knew who that was. All of us slept on him. We were disciples of the East Coast trinity: Nas, Wu-Tang, Mobb Deep. Their imagery was raindrops sliding down lonely windows, the apocalyptic in the mundane. That's New York stuff. DJ Quik, meanwhile, doesn't have time for any of that. He lives in sunny California and it's always a party. You can feel the breeziness in his flow itself. Quik doesn't even rhyme all of his

---

[26] *Pai laew!*: "I'm gone!" (ไปแล้ว)

lines, but sometimes he will, or maybe he'll just brag in free verse for six bars—what's the difference? It's probably a good thing I didn't get into Quik in high school. He would've been a less...what's the word...a less *academic* influence than Nas proved to be.

I arrived at Nim's condo and she met me at the elevator in the lobby. Generally carefree and bursting with giggles, she was in a rare mood tonight. Her dark eyes flashed in anger as she informed me of a particular client's indiscretions. I decided to leave my story for later. Nim worked remotely for a company that helped businesses get loans from banks. I had listened to her explain all the ins and outs to me one night as my eyelids got heavy. My dream recall is better than my memory of financial discussions; I should've taken notes. On this night, she was wearing a button-up blue shirt with hoop earrings, and her nails were polished in alternating colors of yellow, white, and pink. I half-listened as she recounted the business owner's sins.

"Yesterday, you know what she tell me? She say she will have the money *for sure. Mai tung wa*[27] yesterday is the last day and then she will be clear, *chai mai?*"

Nim is from Chonburi, a province down in the central part of Thailand, not far from Bangkok. She came from a family for whom business is written into the DNA with a ballpoint pen. In America, that would merely describe an old family of inherited wealth—the Vanderbilts, for example. Those kids aren't acquainted with the term "no" as anything but a theory.

Nim doesn't come across like that, though. She's a hustler. Nim captained an online clothing store in her spare time, and its success was mostly owing to her own fashion designs. Her professional

---

[27] *Mai tung wa:* "It means that..." (หมายถึงว่ะ)

ventures bore the stamp of her family pedigree yet she hardly came across as conceited, although at times Nim could betray a certain high-bred impatience if we found ourselves at a mismanaged restaurant. Those sort of moments amused me.

She came to the end of her rant, wrapping her arms around me and letting out a weary sigh. I spun threads of her hair around my ring finger and tugged playfully. Suddenly, she pushed me away and looked at me with a scrunched-up face.

"Why you smell like that, na?"

"Huh? *Tum mai*[28]?"

"*Mai chai*, Prism, it smells like *mold*...!" She backed away, bringing her hands up to her nose.

I smelled my t-shirt. *Oh shit, that library book.* I ripped the shirt off, threw it into a corner of the room, and sat down on a chair, once again out of my wits. I was feeling light-headed.

Nim kept asking me what happened. I told her to come sit down and she finally did, still looking offended. Her expression changed to one of shock as I started recounting my tale. As I continued, she stroked her chin and looked at the ceiling.

"Sounds like that library is haunted for sure," she concluded.

"Yeah, with books that smell like sh—"

"And what you think about what they say on the phone? About the instructions?"

"No idea," I sighed, my heart still pounding. "The Thai librarian lady acted like I had to read the book. Super weird. But—oh yeah, I saw the name *Naresuan*. That's all I could see."

"King Naresuan. You know about him?"

"Not really."

"He is the great hero in Thai history. You know when the

---

[28] *Tum mai?*: "Why?" (ทำไม)

Burmese control many places here, right? Long time ago, and King Naresuan, *chai mai*, he fight the Burmese and give Chiang Mai back to the Lanna people." Nim paused to think about it. "Okay, maybe for you, it's sort of like George Washington, right?"

I winced at the comparison. "Ehhh...he was a little different, but yes. I understand."

She cocked her head to the side. "He was the hero in America, *mai chai luh*[29]?"

"Well, yes...but it's complicated."

"Or maybe August Jefferson?"

I gaped at her sincere expression for a moment and started howling. Nim reproached me, somewhat hurt, and I tried to pull myself together. It felt good to let loose. *August Jefferson*. Only in Chiang Mai. I corrected her with cheeks sore from laughter.

"*Nuy jai*[30]," she complained ironically, at the end of her rope.

The moldy shirt remained where it was for the rest of the night. Nim told me she would wash it for me, but that was the last time I ever wore it. After a spontaneous dalliance on the loose cushions of her sofa, Nim gave me one of her oversized t-shirts to wear for sleep. She probably threw away the other one in disgust.

Over the next few days, I replayed the experience at the French library a million and one times in my head. Nothing had ever happened to me like that before. It challenged my imagination in a way I wasn't used to, and I get obsessive with challenges. If there's a bar in a verse I'm recording that doesn't flow right, I might sit for hours 'til I've hit upon the right pattern, discarding hundreds of alternatives. That's just for three lines in a song. This French library thing made my brain curl into a triple pretzel.

---

[29] *Mai chai luh:* "Wasn't he?" (ไม่ไช่เหรอ)

[30] *Nuy jai:* "This is frustrating." (เหนื่อยใจ)

Most respectable people seem to require mathematical proofs to be fulfilled before they entertain the idea of time travel; in other words, they are prejudiced against the idea. The way I see it, if time travel *isn't* possible, that would naturally suggest that "all things" *aren't* possible, which would lead me to the question, how is *anything* possible?

No, I was convinced that I'd gotten a glimpse of 1983, and that didn't bother me in itself. I was more concerned with who the organizers of the trip were. (Hours of *Rick and Morty* episodes had taught me to ask the key questions.) The voice on the phone implied there was something I needed to learn, something for which I needed stern instruction. Why was it important for me, Prism, to learn about some dead Thai military hero? Chiang Mai is a random place, but it had to mean *something*.

I found a six-part Thai film series that had been (over)done on King Naresuan's life and tried watching some of it. He was a prince born during the Burmese occupation of Siam, hundreds of years before the northern and southern halves of the kingdom were made one. The Burmese had ransacked all the principalities—or at least the important ones—and made the Thai governors their vassals. Naresuan grew up in a Burmese court, learned the fine points of military strategy (and cockfighting), returned as king of Phitsanulok, and famously liberated his kingdom and that of Chiang Mai in a single elephant duel. The costuming of the elephants in that one final scene was especially *extra*. They rear their trunks up against their masked faces as they lurch forward, all silk brocades and political pachyderm fury.

One night as I was trying to make heads or tails of all this, I got an out-of-the-blue call from Hop, a chronic texter. I picked up, armed with reasons why I wasn't available to chill.

"Yo, yo, Prism, I need to ask your advice for something, man," he started carefully.

"Sure, what's going on?" Maybe he was sizing up another hot expat girl, as was often the case.

"In Bangkok, have you heard the news about the, ah, how do you say...now there is a pig with *five legs*, yes..." Here Hop paused, refraining to provide context, as if the script of our call required that I react first.

"I've already had dinner, man, sorry," I quipped.

"*Mai kin moo*[31], *chai mai*," Hop snickered appreciatively. "No, you see, this is a...a special pig, because normally...I think this is first pig to have the five legs in one hundred years, yes..."

"Uh-huh?"

"Yes man, it's very amazing, I think." Hop paused again. "Now it will be the time for lottery again soon, I just wonder what your girlfriend think about this pig, man? Will it be lucky for the lottery numbers?"

"A pig with five legs?"

"Yes, *unbelievable*," Hop gushed, not understanding the gist of my remark.

"*Mai chai*, I mean why would that be lucky?"

"I think it's the Thai style, you know," he said thoughtfully. "Anywhere there is strange numbers, there is possibility of fortune. That is the Thai way. We have many stories about this topic, yes. In Bangkok, suppose a pregnant woman have a baby with six toes—she can be very *success* in lottery."

"And what numbers would she play?"

"Maybe the first number is six," Hop explained, "and other numbers are the day baby is born. If the birthday is thirteenth, she can play 613, become very rich, man..."

---

[31] *Mai kin moo:* "You don't eat pork." (ไม่กินหมู)

"Didn't your last girlfriend have six toes?" I teased.

Hop denied the charge good-humoredly before adding, however, that "this might be interesting."

When I asked him if he normally played the lottery, he replied that he hadn't, as it was often a challenge for him to remember calendar dates.

"I am lucky if I wake up before lunch," he informed me.

"So why do you care about the lottery now?"

"When I hear your girlfriend's story, I feel inspiration, and now there is the pig with five legs. I think it is my time, man," Hop concluded fervently.

I saw no reason to contradict his enthusiasm, although there would come a time when I would question his methods. The discussion of fortuitously deformed animals had something of a light-bulb effect on me—I'd forgotten about the Thai mania around lucky numbers, the obsession with the perverse in the search for fortune.

Alone in my kitchen, I fished out some leftover shrimp dumplings and splattered them with cold soy sauce. The sound of a live band drifted from a nearby college bar to my window like the sound of an old radio. I stood there, listening idly. Back in the Carolinas, people tested their luck in the lottery, but I'd never seen such creativity in how luck was conferred upon certain numbers. The Thai lotto player denies no event the interpretation of fortune, however grotesque.

In Nim's case, she hadn't needed to venture into pigstys to find her numbers. She found them provided for her, almost like a service.

The mystery of these events struck me all over again. If the people of Chiang Mai heard about such a person, they would flood her social media in minutes, then probably show up at her doorstep. I winced; that was something I hadn't considered when I filled in Hop.

The next lottery date was around the corner. I still wonder if Nim would've kept playing if she knew what all this was about.

FORM A

It was the day after Visakha Bucha[32], *1983. My uncles and cousins were visiting from Lamphun. They loved to join us on the holidays if it wasn't too rainy. That year I asked* Mae[33] *if we could go see them, but they were so excited for Chiang Mai. It was like a big city to them. We went to Wat Pa Tueng and walked around the pagoda with flowers and incense in our hands. That night, I remember* Pa[34] *took all of us to see a Hong Kong movie in the city. It was at the old Suriwong Theater at Tha Pae Gate. They tore it down a long time ago. Going there was a big deal in those days. Our family lived in San Kampaeng, east of Chiang Mai. We didn't leave San Kampaeng too often. We were simple people. My father sold* nom towhu[35] *and my mother was a seamstress. We had a small farm with chickens. Sometimes my cousins and I would chase them around if we got bored. I am writing this quickly. There are some things that will be left out, but this is to the best of my memory. Some days I think another person's memories live in my head. I remember that my village was in good spirits after* Visakha Bucha. *The sky was clear with pretty white*

---

[32] *Visakha Bucha:* Holiday celebrating the birth, death & enlightenment of Gautama Buddha (วันวิสาขบูชา)

[33] *Mae:* Mother (แม่)

[34] *Pa:* Father (พ่อ)

[35] *Nom Towhu:* Soy milk (นมเต้าหู้)

clouds. I was inside with my mother. She was working on a pair of slacks. I remember hearing a lot of yelling, and we rushed outside. The first person I saw was an old man on his samlor[36], cycling down the road and pointing upward. People were shouting, "Luk ban fai! Luk ban fai[37]!" I looked up too and everything in me froze. It was a ball of fire, like they said, but it looked like a small plane falling out of the sky. I could see it was shaped like a rice plate. I felt like I couldn't move. My eyes were stuck to the ball of fire; I thought it was going to crash in our muban but it was headed in the direction of the big forests. The moment we couldn't see it, we heard a terrible sound that shook our houses like a bomb. After that, everything was silent. The silence was the strangest thing. It was so deep that I thought it would swallow me up. There were no birds chirping, no chickens clucking. I don't know how long I was standing there before Mae picked me up. I was only twelve years old. She took me inside and put me in her bed, and I laid there like that for a long time. I didn't feel scared, or nervous, or anything. My mind was completely blank. I simply knew that everything was different now, everything had changed from the old days for good. I can't tell you how I knew this. There was just an understanding that took the place of my normal thoughts. I know that Pa and some other men went to go find the thing that had crashed. Mae put a wet cloth to my forehead and told me that it was okay, it was a sign from the Buddha after his day of enlightenment. It was a good sign for our village, she said. For a couple of days, everything seemed normal again. The rains came in the mid-morning, and the dirt road outside was veined with little rivers filling in the bike tracks. After the first rain, I would go to the morning market with Mae, just like everyone else. I can still close my eyes and see all the people's faces. Those were my favorite moments. The green smell of the fields filled my nose and the sky looked like a bright painting. People were still talking about the ball of fire, but they didn't want us children to hear. They talked in low voices.

---

[36] *Samlor:* Old three-wheel taxi (สามล้อ)

[37] *Luk ban fai:* Ball of fire (ลูกบาลไฟ)

Soon, their lives would go back to normal, but that wasn't my fate. Sometimes I envy their regular lives, how simple things are for them, how wonderful after the rains to see a smile that you know so well. Later it made me angry and spiteful, it's true. They can't even see the gift they've been given, it was never taken from their hands...but now I'm getting ahead of myself. The first time I floated into the air, I was outside playing with this girl named Ploy. I remember my body suddenly feeling very light, like a feather that could get lost in the wind. I didn't know that my feet were rising off the ground 'til Ploy started screaming. "Ya tum yung ngan! Ya tum yung ngan[38]!" *Startled, I looked down at her. She had a hold of my ankle and was trying to pull me back down. I saw a cat perched on the roof of a house arching its back in alarm. Part of me wanted to keep floating into the sky forever. Something was pulling me up, up, up. When* Mae *rushed out, she started yelling, pulling me down. I collapsed in her arms. I woke up in my bed with everyone around me. The whole village knew what happened. One of the monks from* Wat Pa Tueng *was there, too. He was chanting at my bedside. My parents were pressing down on my arms. They said they didn't want to lose me. This same thing happened two more times, and Ploy's parents stopped letting her come over to play. I started seeing faces around my bed at night. I couldn't see their bodies or anything, just their faces. They were looking at me, blinking their eyes. Sometimes they would stay like that for a long time, other times they just disappeared. I didn't feel anything, I wasn't even scared. Just blank.* Mae *didn't want me to leave my room anymore. I could feel that she didn't know what to do. I knew she hated that feeling. She was always a very sharp person, in charge of our little world. She was scared. I heard her yelling at* Pa *in the morning about the pieces of the machine he found in the forest. She wanted him to throw it away and get it out of our house.* Pa *told her it was important to keep everything for evidence. There was no reason to think that what happened to me was connected to the crash,*

---

[38] *Ya tum yung ngan:* "Stop that!" (อย่าทำอย่างนั้น)

*he said. "*Wen gam[39]*!" she spat in response. One morning there was a knock on the door, followed by male voices that sounded* farang*. I could make out two separate voices, but one spoke more than the other. They were speaking perfect Thai. That sent chills through my body more than anything else. In that time, we rarely met* farangs *who spoke Thai, unless they were missionaries. These men were Americans working with the Thai military. They told* Pa *how they had heard about my "abilities" while they were investigating the crash. We were lucky, the man said. Their superiors were now accepting other children like me into a new program. It was very new and experimental, they informed my father, but they could guarantee a free education, all expenses paid. Children with my "abilities" were now being made a top priority of the State, in the interests of national security. I heard my mother ask them where the school was. They told her I would be taken to a military base in Nakhon Phanom, but that they couldn't give any more information. They would return the next day to hear my parents' decision.* Pa *asked if the ball of fire that crashed in the forest was something from the* manut tang dao[40]*. The Americans said it was better that we didn't know, that they couldn't tell us anyway. The men paid my father 20,000* baht *to hand over the pieces of the machine from the forest. That was a lot of money in those days, and my parents were simple people. When* Mae *came into my room, she found me floating over a meter off my bed, still stretched out on my back. She fell to her knees sobbing.* Pa *ran in and came to a halt at my doorway. He stared at me, hustled to my bedside, and began to wrestle my body down. "*Mai ben rai, luk[41]*," he whispered in my ear. "*Mai ben rai.*" I knew everything was decided then. My parents were simple people.*

---

[39] *Wen gam:* "What bad luck!" (เวรกรรม)

[40] *Manut tang dao:* Aliens (มนุษย์ต่างดาว)

[41] *Mai ben rai, luk:* "Don't worry, child." (ไม่เป็นไร ลูก)

CHAPTER FOUR

In the Thai Kingdom, money comes in many colors, not only green. Green notes are worth twenty *baht*, blue notes fifty *baht*, pink notes one hundred. Five pink notes are equivalent to one purple note. Two purple notes give you a thousand *baht*, or one copper-toned bill. All of them are destined to become leaves on the money trees standing outside of temples made of bamboo sticks and strung with ribbons. Locals grow the money trees until they have ripened with *baht*, festive and floral, ready for harvest. If all of the money were the same color, the trees would fail the Thai standards of beauty, temples would lose funding, and social institutions would fall into ruin. High-minded charity is not an early riser; it has to be tempted out of sleep with the sweetness of bright colors. The *baht* you find in your pocket, then, are the loose pieces of a nationwide, merit-making art project. That's why I told Nim that she had The Purse of Many Colors after her third lottery strike.

This time there was no dream, no voice, no man—only a note on Nim's nightstand that she didn't remember writing. The numbers "221" were scrawled there in Nim's hand. Later that day, another 80,000 *baht* poured out of the Chiang Mai skies. She called me in disbelief and recounted the story. Actually, she *did* have a faint memory of waking up to write something down, but she had no clue as to what caused her to do so. I asked Nim if it was normal for her to wake up out of a dream to take notes. She laughed, shaking her head vigorously on my screen. Her sarcasm could sometimes be mistaken for brief hysteria, which in a weird way I found to be refreshing. Eighty-thousand *baht*, just like that.

There had been some peculiar events the night before, however. Nim and her friend had entered the chic *sois* of the Nimman district for hot-pot and a massage. What they hadn't realized was that a student protest was scheduled to flood the avenues that same evening. Because of certain *lese majeste* laws in place in the kingdom, I am unable to elaborate fully on the target of the students' outrage without risking my legal residency. It is enough to say, perhaps, that the entire establishment had come into question, that there had been something like an abdication of responsibility. Nim was indifferent to the aims of the protests. She shared many of the rebels' opinions but ultimately felt a conservative reverence for Thai tradition. Raised in the colorful shade of the money tree, she saw little reason to uproot it.

Nim and her friend found themselves in the thick of the protests, dodging fists and covering their ears. Big, yellow blobs bobbed on the surface of the crowd; they were inflatable duckies, used by the students to shield themselves from the law's high-pressure hoses. ("It's all a goddamn cartoon," Gabe would probably say.) The two women, both in heels, shuffled closer to their prized hot-pot, and the crowd began to thin. This is where things got strange. Nim happened to turn her head over her left shoulder and found her gaze returned. There was a tall man in a business suit standing motionless amid the crush of students, staring directly at her. His hands were thrust in his pockets, and he appeared impervious to the ruckus around him.

"You know," Nim said, "he stand right in front of the people who do the protest, but it looked like nobody saw him, and he just look at me. I think we were friends from before, but I never know him."

The sudden flash of an apparent meteor in the sky only complicated matters; the students, fearing some kind of attack, fled in every direction, and the pair of friends finally ducked into their restaurant. Once inside, Nim and her companion seemed to lose interest in everything they'd witnessed; such is the comfort of Chiang Mai hot-pot establishments. Even so, Nim hadn't seen the strange man for the last time that evening. She spotted him once again in the parking garage of her condo after her friend had departed. This time, he was walking briskly in the other direction, his face turned back toward her in the manner of someone saying goodbye.

"Was it the same guy you saw before?"

"*Chai,* I think so, but I still can't see his face."

"Did he have a mask on or something?"

"*Mai chai,* but I don't know how to explain—when I try to focus on his face, I can't see any details. *Yang mai hen arrai luy[42].*"

"You didn't take a picture?!"

"Prism!"

"And you think you know him from somewhere?"

"Yes, maybe. But I don't know how I can think that. We've never met before, but I can feel that he knows me very well. *Nang[43]* Nim, *Nang* Nim, what happened to you," she added plaintively to herself.

"Well at least this guy isn't only haunting *my* house," I said out

---

[42] *Yang mai hen arrai luy*: "I still can't see anything." (ยังไม่เห็นอะไรเลย)

[43] *Nang*: "Little sister." (น้อง)

loud to myself. Nim's attention was already reclaimed by her phone.

They say you never forget a face, but I wondered how you could recall one you'd never seen. This man of mystery didn't appear to be hemmed in by the usual boundaries of reality; it seemed just as likely that he'd appear in a DMT hallucination as he would on the street corner next to a *somtam*[44] stand. As such, I had to consider whether or not his anonymity should be a source of apprehension. Was it possible to be a time-traveling bank robber, executing heists across the time-space continuum to beat inflation? I had no idea. Despite the high weirdness, it was hard to argue with cash money, regardless of the currency or economic era.

Three consecutive wins in any lottery was unheard of. Any Thai person, for example, has roughly a one-percent chance of winning money in any given raffle. Normally, they would need to play ten thousand times to average *one* win at that probability. Nim had now hit three winning lottery numbers in only three attempts. It gets even zanier when you consider that the probability she could win multiple times within ten attempts is *two ten-thousandths* of a percent. Whoever this mysterious dude actually was, he was helping Nim break statistics with a two-by-four. Beyond that, we knew nothing.

Given the vacuum of information, along with the clearly super-natural element, it was easy for me to project interpretations born from the death of my mother. Since her passing, I'd had experiences that seemed to indicate her continued existence at a "different address," as I heard one psychic put it. I don't often share these experiences, as I've noticed that many seem to take them as an invitation to suggest an "explanation," as though anything running counter to their worldview needs immediate resolution. Speaking

---

[44] *Somtam:* Papaya salad (ส้มตำ)

for myself, I am content to live in a world I don't understand. Any form of comprehension is momentary and accidental.

My mother had managed to communicate two out of three things to me from the other side. One, that she had accepted a position in the afterlife that involved looking out for me; and two, that her presence would be known by the appearance of tiger butterflies. The first communication, I guess, didn't necessarily surprise me—it invokes the sentimentality of two souls whispering promises in the hour of parting. Her language of employment was curious enough, but I didn't give it much thought. After I received my mother's message, however, there was a general surge of tiger butterflies around me, looping my path at almost every turn, scattering across my balcony like tiny embers. Every walk in nature bore the inevitability of their appearance.

As for her third communication, I was still waiting for it to resolve itself, though I could hardly imagine how it ever could. Night after night, I found myself watching my mother's figure approaching me, holding something outstretched in her hand. It was a rose-colored gift box with the lid positioned at a crooked angle. She would draw nearer and nearer until the gift box seemed ready to lose its lid. I began to coil myself in anticipation of catching it and viewing the box's contents. In this moment, of course, I was the sum of all my childhood delights and dependencies, only existing to receive my mother's kindness. But this gave way in the next moment to a feeling of fatherly concern—she was now a little girl, looking up at me. That was when the cloud of fog enveloped us. The last thing I would see were her blue eyes glowing in the whiteness, dew-drops of prescience at dream's end.

Whatever was in this rose-colored gift box, I assumed it to be of tremendous value. After all, my mother was carving out time in her busy afterlife schedule to give it to me. Only, it wasn't quite working out. Somehow we kept getting interrupted, just as the Wi-Fi always drops out at a critical point in Zoom calls. Or, conversely, was that in itself the greater message—the idea that something was preventing her transmission; something which, perhaps, I could control? One of my friends in the spoken-word scene likes to joke that the answer to any problem is "meditate more." (That friend also has a bigger budget for crystals than I do for rent, but that's another story.) A third alternative, I told myself, was that I had *already* received the gift. I just had to recognize it for what it was on my own.

As my girlfriend collected more riches through the Thai lottery, I had to ask myself if it was a coincidence. After all, was I not in-directly benefiting from the opulent dining, the occasional free pair of sneakers? That's not to mention Nim's sunnier, more stress-free mood, or what I liked to call her "lottery glow." These were all superlatively *nice* things, yet something told me that the value of the contents of that rose-colored gift box exceeded online Adidas vouchers. My mother was drawing my attention to something else, perhaps a code whose potential glittered at my birth. What was required to access it? These uncertainties greeted me each morning like the smell of Akha Ahma coffee beans. I felt lured into a pursuit that I didn't fully understand.

After receiving Nim's lottery updates, I was overcome with an urge to eat a Thai rice porridge dish called *jok*[45]. The flavor, if you'll excuse the pun, is anything but. A foreigner hasn't fully become assimilated until he starts craving local dishes that can't be found in Thai restaurants back home. The stomach is the first to become fluent in the language of an unfamiliar land, then the tongue fol-lows. I've always had this hackneyed theory that a person's fluency

---

[45] *Jok:* Thai rice porridge (โจ๊ก)

in Thai correlates to the amount of regional Thai food they eat. There's a certain amount of *nam prik*[46] one has to consume (and release) before he can dabble in the tonal adventures of Thai expression. A bilingual stomach is key to literacy; the most anyone could say about this theory is that it's difficult to disprove.

That craving for *jok* on my part was preceded by a more random urge to drive to the Mae Hia market. My stomach, having a detailed food map of Chiang Mai stored in its cells, perked up at the idea and asserted its opinion. I found myself driving south on the empty highway before I'd really figured out why I was doing so. There were many places to eat closer to my house, even at that time of night. Mae Hia is around fifteen minutes south of the town proper. The highway travels in both directions, separated by a shallow canal—in the daytime, the green domes of the mountain range glow to the west but are veiled after sundown, when the power of their presence is felt in other channels of perception. By motorbike, you pass through a sudden temperature barrier, on the other side of which the air is chill and nearly aquatic. Rows of streetlamps keep the darkness of the mountains at bay.

I certainly wasn't expecting to see anyone I knew at Mae Hia, not at that time of night. Some Thai places have a force field preventing foreigners from entering after dark. Mae Hia market was one of them. In fact, calling Mae Hia a market is only partially accurate, given how we interpret the term. It's more like an improbable enclave of shops and businesses orbiting an island of fresh produce. In one lineup of stores alone, you have an option of drinking chili-flavored coffee, trying on new glasses, or seeing a gynecologist. On one wing is a Lego-themed daycare, and on the other is a massage shop whose one-hour service is cheaper than a

---

[46] *nam prik:* Notoriously spicy Thai chili sauce. (น้ำพริก)

burger. Mae Hia made plazas look bothersome—the people here don't require boundaries between their domains of pursuit; all needs are collapsed into one localized life experience. That suits my brain better somehow.

At night, the shops shut down and the center of gravity shifts to a constellation of street vendors on the edge of the road, filling the air with the spices of *kuy tiew*[47] or the egginess of banana *rotis*[48]. I was wandering between the little stands when suddenly I noticed Open Source gesturing to me from a plastic table, arms spread out to either side. Source never seemed like he belonged in a northern Thai setting; it was more like New York City had become a super-nova, exploded, and this particular human was one of its fragments that landed on the other side of the planet. He was wearing a blue Georgetown hoodie, baggy sweat shorts, and a radiant pair of Jordan 3s. His temples were graced with the lines of a barber's razor, but his eyes showed a touch of tiredness. We dapped up, I ordered some *jok*, sat down, and there I was with the man of missed appointments himself.

"Where you been hiding, man?" That's what he always said.

"In plain sight, I guess."

"Fuckin' touché, Mr. Prism, the hot-spitter," he laughed. "You heard that new Fabolous mixtape?"

"*Fabolous?* You mean ol' F-A-B-O…?"

"Bro, album of the year. It's a must-cop! I had to Macgyver my iTunes account, it kept logging me out and asking me to verify my identity, it was *ludicrous,* man. How do they expect me to remember my cousin's street name when I'm rolling a blunt?"

"My question is who would put their cousin's street name for

---

[47] *kuy tiew:* Standard Thai noodle soup. (ก๋วยเตี๋ยว)
[48] *Rotis:* Pan-fried bread with condensed milk. (โรตี)

identity verification?" I shot back with a grin.

"A certified chronic blunt-smoker, that's who!"

I joined in with his laughter; it was always impossible not to. Source had this amazing skill of pulling you in with self-deprecating anecdotes. For all I know, the thing about a new Fabolous mixtape could've been an invention on his part (I never checked).

"The hell are you eating bro, rice soup?" Source demanded affectionately. "Looks like some poverty-porridge...we gotta get you back on those steaks and filet mignons!"

I lazily remonstrated, shaking my head as my teeth caught on a slice of ginger.

"Listen, Prism, I have to get back to the crib and see my babies. Let me talk to you for a sec. We got a show coming up at this spot called Topic 36 near the river. You been? Come through and get on the mic, we need an extra MC. Thursday from eight to midnight."

"Who's spinning for y'all?"

"Man, DJ Concise, who else?"

"What's up with all that drum-n-bass he does, though?"

"*All that drum-n-bass.* C'mon, Prism, you're telling me people will show up for *only* rap? That's not how it is anymore, man. We do our rap thing for an hour, drinks get to flowing, then the drum-n-bass comes on when everyone is blitzed."

"Freestyles? Writtens?"

"It's whatever, G. Hit 'em with those Prism bars, free 'em from the prison bars!" A stud in Source's left ear caught the light as he threw his head back in laughter. He made to go.

"Source," I interjected, detaining him, "you ever hear about a ghost helping people win the lottery?"

He stood there as I summarized Nim's strange success story. His jovial expression became clouded with concern.

"Bro," he intoned solemnly, adjusting his bag's chest strap, "I would be very careful with anything like that. Very fuckin' careful—for real! You know about the djinn spirits, don't you?"

"Like the *Arabian Nights* kinda thing?"

Source shook his head, scornful of my reference. "This is real life, man. I personally know people...look, you can get locked into a contract without even realizing it. All you have to do is accept something they give you; then it's over. They got you."

"What do djinn spirits look like?" I asked. "This one's face is blurred but he has nice taste in business suits."

Source took a grave sigh. "It don't matter what they look like, man, it's how they manipulate you. What is your girl doing with the money?"

"Nothing yet. But this guy hasn't said anything about a contract."

"There's a cost to everything," Source reminded me, dapping me up in parting. "Just remember that, family. Let me know about Thursday, yeah?" A man of the party, his moralism always took me by surprise.

I turned my face to the half-finished bowl of *jok*, spooning out chunks of fried onion. Whenever I get invited to perform somewhere, I feel a glow of privilege, followed by an inclination to find a petty excuse to ghost the whole thing. Source's voice rose into the air again, and I looked up. He was walking back toward me and stopped when he had my attention.

"Yo, look up the song 'Rosecrans' by DJ Quik! Think of some Chiang Mai rhymes. We're gonna make a hit just like that one."

There I was, caught in the snare of Source's persuasion again. Of course I knew the Quik song he was talking about—it was a mellow blur of strings, keys, and loked-out synths over a Sunday-slow drum pattern, a casual ode to Compton. I had composed some slapdash lines to this instrumental already. The random Source encounter had the appearance of an alignment, but I refused to see it as anything but a red herring. I had no interest in having my expectations inflated for another musical mirage (or so I thought). My phone started going off as I paid for the bowl of *jok*; it was Nim.

"Prism, *yuu nai nia[49]*?"

"Mae Hia, *krub. Tum mai*?"

"You remember the story I tell you? About seeing the lotto guy at the protest? Yes, and I also tell you about the bright light in the sky, *chai mai*?"

"Oh, right, the meteor?"

"Yes, but I want to tell you something, Prism. My friend showed me a video of that night—*jing jing[50] na* I think it's not really a meteor."

Nim sent me the video and I squinted at my screen. If what I was seeing *was* a meteor, then I was even more ignorant of astronomy than I thought. The clip ended with a big yellow duckie blocking the camera. I dragged the slider to rewind ten seconds, watched again, and whistled in disbelief.

---

[49] *Yuu nai nia:* "Where are you?" (อยู่ไหนเนี่ย)

[50] *Jing jing:* "For real" (จริงๆ)

FORM B

No one told me they would take the sky away from me. I guess it wasn't an important detail. In San Kamphaeng, I never thought about the sky so much. It was always just there, being itself. I used to imagine how long my arms would have to be to hug the sky, to hold it in my arms. Those days were gone. Now my world was four white walls, a mattress, and a table. There was no blue sky, just fluorescent lights that gave me a headache. The sky was dead and so was I. There were only the men in uniform. They never smiled. I wondered if they were dead, too. Every day they brought me khou man kai[51] *and* cha tai[52] *for breakfast, lunch, dinner.* Eee hia![53] *I even had to wait for them to take me to the bathroom. I kept thinking of the* luk ban fai *outside my house. It had made me a prisoner. The military men had brought me to Nakhon Phanom in a jet plane with an American flag on the side. It was my first time on a plane. I never thought about how tiny people were until I saw the view from my window. The rice fields fit together like chess squares and the trucks were insects crawling through them. I always thought* Pa *and* Mae *were so, so big, as big as the sky. Now I saw how tiny they were, and they didn't matter to me*

---

[51] *Khou man kai:* Rice and chicken dish (ข้าวมันไก่)

[52] *Cha tai:* Thai tea (ชาไทย)

[53] *Eee hia!:* "Shit!" (อีเหี้ย)

anymore. That's what I told myself when the tears came those first nights. Mae *always took me on her lap and braided my hair when I was upset. She wiped my tears and sang old songs from* Isaan. *I never knew what memories were 'til I stayed in the room with four white walls. I saw they were worse than dreams. They made me feel things that weren't there. I tried to stop remembering and my mind went blank. When the plane first landed at the air force base, my feet didn't want to touch the ground. I tried going down the staircase, but my feet were walking on air. I was falling into the sky again. There were five or six military men around me and they started laughing, only laughing. One of them grabbed my ankle and yanked me down to the landing strip. Another tilted my head back and squirted something into my mouth from a dropper. That was the last time I ever floated off the ground. The men acted like it was a big joke. Two of them were* farangs *and their breath stank of cigarettes. "Don't piss off Wonder Woman,"* they said. Piss off, piss off. *I didn't understand what it meant for a long time but I knew that I hated it. The Thai men in uniforms were mostly quiet and listened to the* farangs. *They led me to a long building with a flat roof. The air was hot with jet fuel and it filled my lungs until I felt dizzy. I heard the Thai men say that my training as a* ma du[54] *would start soon. That's when I started vomiting and blacked out. I don't know for how long. When I woke up, my chin was bumping against someone's shoulder. They were carrying me through a long, empty hallway. I tried to jump out of the man's arms but my body couldn't move.* Rang kai kong chan mai chua fang[55]. *I thought that my body must still be sleeping, or maybe I was still sleeping and everything was a nightmare. That was when I saw the other girl. She was standing in a doorway with other men in uniform around her. I still see her eyes looking at me before I go to sleep, before I wake up, in the darkness in between. She was eleven or twelve, like me. Her eyes were sunken*

---

[54] *Ma du:* Witch or prophetess (หมอดู)
[55] *Rang kai kong chan mai chua fang:* "My body disobeyed."
(ร่างกายของฉันไม่เชื่อฟัง)

and her hair was straggly. Khon purma[56], *I guessed. Her eyes locked with mine and never looked down, even as we got farther away. She started to lift her little hand in my direction. That's when the men hustled her out of sight and slammed the door. The hallway was empty again except for the door's echo. I couldn't stop thinking of her after that. Everything had been taken from me, and she was all I had. Maybe she was like me, another poor little Wonder Woman. We could fly in the air,* jing jing, *but couldn't even comb our own hair.* Na song san[57]. *I made up stories in my head about her past, about adventures we would take together. She became my secret sister without there ever having been a word spoken between us. I began to think she could hear my thoughts and see my dreams, and when we floated over rivers and temples together, I saw them as her ideas just as much as my own. The things that happened to me next only convinced me of this further. After what I thought was forever, a Thai admiral entered the four white walls one day, along with one of the* farangs. *I had seen him before. He had a lean, hard face with a red nose and neatly cropped white hair. In his hand, he held a little bottle of chocolate milk. He raised it in my direction and grinned. The Thai admiral told me that if I completed a day of training, they would let me have one sip, maybe even two. If I listened to them, he said, I could become a* ma du *and help them find the bad guys. I was confused and scared. I couldn't understand what they meant. The admiral held a folding chair at his side and put it down for the* farang. *He sat down, crossed his legs, and said his name was P[58] Tom. He wore an orange Hawaiian shirt and his arms were hairy. With one finger, he touched his head, then made a circle in the air. They told me my mind could go anywhere in space and time. If I could help them find their targets, I could have all the chocolate milk I wanted. I asked them when I could go home—I didn't care about any other space or time. The admiral translated for P Tom. The*

---

[56] *Khon purma:* Burmese person (คนพม่า)

[57] *Na song san:* Pitiful (น่า สงสาร)

[58] *P:* A title of respect for elders (พี่)

farang *slid his chair closer to me and looked me in the face. "Your home is with us now, Wonder Woman," he said. I started crying. The admiral scolded me and said I didn't know how lucky I was. P Tom waved the bottle of chocolate milk under my nose. "Don't you want some?" I wiped my tears with my sleeve and nodded. "We're going to help you use your psychic skills in the real world, that's all," he said. P Tom reached into his breast pocket and slid a photograph across the table in front of me. It was a middle-aged man dressed in a military uniform, smiling. "This is our friend, Khun Sa," they told me. "We want you to play a game. Close your eyes and try to see where he lives. Concentrate!" I have to end this entry soon. Secrecy is of the utmost importance. Of course I saw everything in my mind...orchid gardens, strawberry fields, a one-story concrete house surrounded by soldiers, machine guns...P Tom was very pleased. When S. first appeared to me later that night, she said it was strange how drug kingpins always had the nicest smiles. "Maybe it's because they have so many friends in high places," she added with a wink. When she opened the door, she was holding fresh roses in her hands. She stood there for a long time, looking at me and saying nothing. I was looking at a short Thai woman in military uniform with her hair pulled back. Something was different about her. The woman's eyes roved the room. She stepped forward, placed the roses on the table, then picked up the empty bottle of chocolate milk in the corner and put it in the waste bin. "Call me S., kha." She looked at my face and made a sound in her throat. Fumbling through her bag, she pulled out some baby wipes and cleaned under my eyes and nose. S. told me that she worked at the French embassy in Chiang Mai, near the river. When I asked about the roses, she gave me a quiet smile.*

CHAPTER FIVE

There's something I neglected to mention about the beginning of my relationship with Nim. If I could trace the forging of our connection back to one moment, one conversation, it would likely be when we mutually forgot the exact same character in not only *Harry Potter* but also *The Fresh Prince of Bel-Air*. A remarkably millennial romance, I know—built on the illusory edifice of telecasts, touching a neon sky. I had convinced Nim to take a short road trip with me to Chiang Rai, an old Lanna settlement near the Burmese border. I pressed her to join and, despite some initial resistance on her part, we were soon following twisting roads through the mountains in a rental car.

I've heard of all kinds of outlandish criteria for a romantic partner—the shape of her feet, the way he holds chopsticks, the type of emojis frequently used in texts (too bubbly, too passive-aggressive, a little crude).

Most of these things I've never dreamed of, nor can I discern what kind of feet are sexy and which are not. My only concern usually boils down to this: *Can we travel well together?* If she can handle my spontaneity, my contempt for plans, my unpredictable absorptions, I'm happy. And so I invited Nim on a three-day trip to

Chiang Rai to see if our status as lovers was certified. (It was.)

The situation went like this. We'd arrived in Chiang Rai the night before and were driving thirty miles out of town to visit Doi Mae Salong, a mountain chain of mist-laden valleys and tea plantations overseen by descendants of the Chinese Kuomintang soldiers who notoriously fought communism with heroin sales. Our little Toyota climbed its way through virginal meadows, and we put our windows down to let the fresh mountain air in. I felt Nim's hand close around mine. Freed from Chiang Mai's vortex of commitments, our conversation was looser and more callous. Soon it became incredibly important to remember all of the characters in *Harry Potter.*

"Who is that nerdy guy, na? He always with Harry in Gryffindor."

"You mean Ron Weasley?"

"*Mai chai*, I mean the nerdy guy."

"Ron is pretty nerdy, though."

"Prism! *Mun ben eek khon*[59]. Ron have red hair, but not so nerdy like the other guy."

"I gue—oh, you mean the guy who fell off his broom?"

"Yes! What's his name?"

We had reached a familiar impasse. Nim set aside her bag of seaweed chips to reach for her phone, but I grabbed her wrist with my free hand, protesting in laughter. Sometimes our dependence on search engines bothers me. I, of course, was alone in this misgiving. Nim glared at me, the bangs on her forehead flaring out in the breeze. I gave in. Moments later, the answer came.

"Neville Longbottom!"

Her Thai tongue turned the *v* into a *w* and adorably shuffled the

---

[59] *Mun ben eek khon:* "It's another person." (มันเป็นอีกคน)

syllable stresses, giving an air of class to the name's posterior. "How could we forget?" I hooted in laughter.

The road opened up to panoramas of green sloping valleys that cupped the midday sun in silence. Nim instinctively pressed her palms together in reverence as we passed a spirit house partially concealed in shadows of brush. In Asian cultures, it isn't a contradiction to be at once business-minded and superstitious. Most Thai businesses, in fact, wouldn't exist without the preliminary calculations of an astrologer. Yes, there should've been a greater distance between us than there was; fifty years ago, it's a small chance that an American man and a Thai woman would share knowledge of the same movie, let alone that their minds would select to forget the same character. Soon, conversation turned (naturally?) to the Fresh Prince.

"Will is such a crazy guy," Nim chuckled, examining her lipstick in the pull-down mirror. "I try to make the handshake like he do with my friend...*psssshhh!*...you know, right? But I think it's difficult for us," she concluded ruefully.

"I can teach you," I offered with a grin.

"Really," she demanded, pausing the application of her lipstick to shoot me a critical up-down look. I indulged in the mental image of two Thai women fumbling to perform an ultra-smooth dap-up like early '90s rap stars. It was too good. I began reciting the Fresh Prince's legendary opening theme.

"Prism, you can rap the whole song *luh*[60] *kha?*"

"Of course." I gladly acquiesced, reaching over to pinch her chin at all the key punchlines (and risking a bitten finger).

"I *chob*[61] Hillary, na. Hillary Banks," Nim asserted at the end.

---

[60] *Luh:* Verbal question mark (เหรอ)

[61] *Chob:* "Like" (ชอบ)

"Oh, yeah? Why?"

Nim affected a sing-song tone as she delivered the clichés. "She's so pretty, *hi-so*[62], cool fashion. Not care anything about stupid guys. *Yim luy*[63]!"

I fought back a Hillaryesque eye roll. This was—well, *you* know—the most infuriating character on the show, a ditzy primadonna of post-Reagan America. It was very on-brand, though, for a normal Thai person to fall for the light-skinned star. The irony of Hillary Banks' attitude flew over Nim's head; the instrument of that irony—H.B.'s sexiness—was all that mattered.

"Ehh, I liked her sister more," I commented.

"Oh, she's cute too, na!"

"Wait, what was her name?"

We confirmed our mutual amnesia with a glance. "*Eek laew*[64]!" Nim chirped, sighing dramatically and shaking her head. We had named off all the other favorites: Geoffrey, Carlton, Uncle Phil, Jazz—even *Aunt Vivian*. I knit my brow and searched Nim's eyes. Her swift hands went to her phone and excavated the forgotten meme; it was Ashley Banks, *of course*. There's a tawdry elation in recalling pop trivia, like a street drug that pumps your heart rate for five minutes before evaporating. The familiar images dance across our brains but there's little else to say. In the past, comradery was driven by shared religious beliefs, worship of the same deities. I suppose you could say not much has changed, except that our gods and goddesses have become easier to forget.

There was a bend in the road and a sudden, colorful vision greeted our eyes. A troupe of Akha Ama hill tribe women was

---

[62] *Hi-so:* A colloquial abbreviation of "high society" (ไฮโซ)

[63] *Yim luy:* "So cool!" (ยิ้มเลย)

[64] *Eek laew:* "Again!" (อีกแลว)

milling around stalls of trinkets and scarves along the side of the road, their mountain-worn faces smiling in the sun. All of them wore red ornamental headdresses and woven sashes hung with beads, shells, and tassels that matched the pattern of their leggings. They waved at us as I slowed to admire their artistry. Their beauty wasn't broadcast to the other side of the world, nor were they a currency on the global market of small talk. It was only *here* they existed, and nowhere else.

There was a time, of course, when the tender white buds of Akha opium became cheap heroin in the streets of New York, Baltimore, and Detroit, a time when the tribe's innocence was a key asset to the international drug trade. They were courted, used, and abandoned. Nothing personal, of course, just the machinery of globalization at work—the very thing that made it possible for me to live in Chiang Mai, the same phenomenon, too, that allowed a Thai woman from Chonburi to be as familiar with the Fresh Prince as I was, creating a situation in which I found myself *more* attracted to her in some bizarre, inexplicably modern way. Our mutual memory glitch had aphrodisiacal qualities. As such, Neville Longbottom and Ashley Banks will always be holy characters in my book, in ways that are hard for others to understand.

Later that afternoon, we enjoyed the cloud-swept views of terraced tea plots from a Chinese teahouse, talking of nothing in particular. There were no CIA agents, no lines of pack mules with bundles of heroin strapped across their backs; only hot cups of *oolong*[65] offered with a bow. We, too, were innocent; innocent of any foreknowledge of what our union was supposed to mean. I went back to the Akha women to make an obligatory tourist purchase, in this case a handwoven teal-and-purple striped hoodie.

---

[65] *Oolong:* Chinese green tea (อูหลง)

The numbers "221" were scrawled across the inside tag, something we'd only notice with interest much later.

It was the day of the show at Topic 36 with Source and DJ Concise. Nim was composing her second face at the bathroom mirror, an unknowable row of small bottles lining the sink like a set of paints. I don't think (straight) men fully appreciate the supreme act of creativity that young women require themselves to perform in order to meet the unwritten criteria of beauty. They recreate the Mona Lisa every morning, eyes half-closed, even, while men like me give nary a thought to the genius blazing in our midst. She won my approval largely by remaining recognizable. That's typically as far as my recognition goes.

The sun was dancing across the veranda as my eyes lazily roamed the clouds, the mountains, the day's new shade of blue above. I was half-listening to Nim's chatter through the screen door. Horns of a Smokey Robinson song layered themselves over the voices of my Thai neighbors below. I knew those horns from DJ Quik's *Rhythmalism* album well but had never sought the original sample ('til I heard it by pure chance). Sample-chasing is an infinite pursuit. Just retracing one great producer's credits can take you across the span of modern music. They say hip-hop is derivative, that it didn't create anything new, *blah blah blah*. It's not true—hip-hop invented a new strain of déjà vu. How else can you describe the experience of hearing a sound you already know, but in a context that's completely unfamiliar? Every track is an atomic series of trapdoors, each of which leads to another world of a genre. You only catch a glimpse, but that glimpse primes you for what will later be full, ecstatic immersion. Thus one is led from DJ Quik to Smokey Robinson, horn-dazed in remembrance.

More trapdoors were starting to appear in my own reality. I had come to anticipate Nim's reports with a zeal that few other things in my life inspired. Lately, the strangest tales had been rolling from her tongue. Her nonchalance about everything gave me the sense that *I* was striking the lottery as much as she was. I had waited all my life to hear these stories, I realized. Was I hearing them simply for that reason, or had that desire on my part been a kind of premonition? It was impossible to say. My brain was a perfect environment for doubts to sprout, grow, and prosper. Still, they always wilted at Nim's words, just as they always evaporate at the moment my hand touches the mic.

There was a UFO story from the night of the protests circulating on Pantip—the Thai Reddit—that had apparently gone viral. That was how Nim's friend had discovered the video of the explosion of lights over Nimman, followed by what looked to be some kind of saucer that streaked diagonally into the distance. A forty-two-year-old man from Lamphun, in town for business, claimed to have been contacted by alien visitors less than five minutes after the explosion, somewhere in the industrial block known as Chang Puak. There were no other witnesses. In his original post on Pantip, the man reported hearing a whistling sound behind him. Turning around, he saw a tall, wispy shadow that moved like "living smoke" across the pavement. The man heard a voice in his head assuring him of his safety. For what he calculated to be five minutes, which he admitted could have easily been more or less, the shadow described how it came from a superior race, then proceeded to give the poor man what it claimed was a formula to "have the universe at his fingerprints" (or fingertips?). The man described this formula to the police then promptly forgot it once the report had been filled, save that every person had enough knowledge to "make him a deathless god of love." Other Pantip posters had immediately contacted the local police department. The document was still "under review," they were told. I found it amusing that the local Chiang Mai police, that ragtag group of strongmen who made their money from ambushing motorcyclists at cleverly-placed checkpoints, had suddenly stumbled into the secret of the universe and thus put our whole Milky Way at their mercy. Nim chuckled as she recalled some of the replies on Pantip.

"One person say that if *tom ruat*[66] have the power to teleport, we will only see them at three places: traffic light, lady bar, happy massage!" I urged her to continue. "Another person say if you be the snitch on mafia, there will be a problem, so what happens if you be the snitch on alien?" I agreed that it was a conundrum. "Prism, maybe you want to join this group. *Khou ja aow tent pai Chiang Puak tuk khun!*[67] Maybe they think the aliens will come back there, na."

If that polluted part of the city made the same impression on them that it did me, we'd all probably be waiting in vain.

"What about your lottery man," I interjected. "All of this happened on the same night as the protests, right? I don't get it."

"Uhh." The universal Thai sound of commiseration that also tells you there is nothing left to say. *You're right, but let's drop it.* Once those iron bars go up, there's not much you can do to pry them open. The topic gets changed, and the ensuing conversation is a draft that blows you into a different hemisphere.

"Prism, you hear the news about Malila?" An acceleration of clattering in the bathroom signaled that Nim's beautification ritual was coming to a close.

Malila, Malila. A sweet name, and one that I openly loathed;

---

[66] *Tom ruat:* Police (ตำรวจ)

[67] *Khou ja aow tent pai Chiang Puak tuk khun:* "They'll set up tents in Chang Puak every night!" (เขาจะเอาเต็นท์ไปช้างเผือกทุกคืน)

Nim always pretended not to take notice. Malila was her idol, the one whose videos Nim watched with more devotion than any other channel. Malila was the Thai DIY makeup guru and entrepreneur of great acclaim—in every video, she famously wore a hair bow with triangle cat ears over an innocent pixie cut. In fact, I'm pretty sure she had the silhouette trademarked.

Five seconds of one of her videos was enough to leave me nauseated. Her personality was typical for Thai social media: saccharine-sweet, overly feminized, cloying, fickle, fragile as a set of china. As Malila caked her face in whitening products and made her lips a chic off-mocha, she boldly mixed in tales of female perseverance with her vanity. Not that I'm against the independence of women in any way: rather, it was the shallow ploy of marketing herself as a victim, with all the usual clichés of suffering and hardship, that left me sickly-green in the face; the idea that her skin-deep products had more meaning simply because she could crib the language of an Oprah guest. This was one of those things I had to bite my tongue on, obviously. Malila was sacrosanct.

"She announced on her Twitter that soon will have grand opening for new business. Do you know what is it?"

I groaned and began rolling up some tobacco.

"Guess," Nim teased, enjoying my irritation.

"A women-only shopping mall? I don't know."

"Nope. Malila's *Karsai*[68] Massage Parlor. She will open first locations in Bangkok, Phuket, Chiang Mai."

"Huh? Isn't that the massage where they…"

"Yep. Special massage for man, from the Tantra. Prism *chob chai mai?*"

I almost choked on the inhale and went into a fit of coughing.

---

[68] *Karsai*: Traditional form of genital therapy (กษัย)

That was a bit of news I hadn't been prepared for at all. "Why the hell would Malila open a shop for pleasuring some creepy dudes all day? Isn't that against everything she talks about in those videos?"

"Many Thai people are angry about that too," Nim admitted. "But Malila say she isn't a person in the sex industry—she say *karsai ben prapani tang sassana*[69], yes, and that she want to reeducate man, teach him how to use sex energy to, uh...Prism, how to say? *Hai kan raksa*[70]."

"Oh, come on, are you serious? So giving us hand jobs is going to teach us how to heal the world?"

"Prism! Karsai is not a hand job, it's *therapy for man*," she chided. The screen door swung open and Nim stepped out onto the veranda for her debut, the transformation finally complete. A red pullover cardigan, unbuttoned, matched her generously applied lipstick, while her shower of dark hair framed cheekbones that shone like a painted easel. The lettered white tee and blue denim gave you the idea that a director on a movie set had instructed her to dress "casual."

"...therapy f-for men, yes," I stammered, flicking the cigarette away.

"Ta-daaa," she giggled, twirling around. "*Suay mai*[71]?"

"Tell me more about that therapy," I grinned, resting one hand on her waist and nibbling her ear with ill-concealed intentions. Nim, however, pushed me out of the heavenly circumference of perfume with two hands.

---

[69] *Karsai ben prapani tang sassana:* "Karsai is a religious custom." (กษัยเป็นประเพณีทางศาสนา)

[70] *Hai kan raksa:* "Give healing." (ให้การรักษา)

[71] *Suay mai:* "Am I beautiful?" (สวยไหม)

"What therapy? I think you can do yourself. *Som nam na*[72]!"

Nim followed that up by telling me I needed to get ready, decisively banishing any other ideas in my head. It was crazy how she could tell me what to do without being bossy. All my life, I'd hated taking orders from just about anyone, even my parents sometimes. I fiercely protected my right to laziness. Nim was the first partner I had who made me *want* to be told what to do. It was like she was filling a void in my life by doing so. *Prism, you need to go to immigration. Prism, why haven't you done your laundry?* It was Nim's gentle nature that helped me accept her subtle tyrannies, her mumbled mandates. (It also helped that she said *na* after everything.) I guess sometimes when you're lost, you need someone to remind you of obligations, things to do. It persuades you into believing that the day ahead is worth living.

It's weird: in reconstructing all these events, I find myself attaching different meanings to each one, which are more in reference to where everything was leading rather than how I experienced them in the moment. It might sound bad, but I never gave my relationship with Nim much thought—not as it was happening. It just *was*. Only in retrospect have I taken an interest in digging deeper, collecting fragments to piece together a mosaic that I already know, on some level, exists in perfect completion.

I remember that on this very same night, after everything that happened at the show, I got a random text from an ex-girlfriend with whom I was still close. She was referencing the Nas line from *Stillmatic* about the dead bird and shattered sky. What did I think it meant? I told her that I didn't think there was a meaning; or rather, it was one of those poetic moments that could mean anything. It was only later that I decided I was wrong in saying that. The dead

---

[72] *Som nam na:* A way of mocking a friend's plight (สมน้ำหน้า)

bird was past relationships, the shattered sky that realm of expectations by which those relationships defined themselves. Not just
the romantic kind, either—relationships with our fathers and
mothers, too. Who can say what Nas intended to mean at that moment? My own life made it mean what I needed it to.

So in saying that, how can I possibly know what this story will
mean to any particular person, or someone, perhaps, who sees the
mosaic more clearly than I do? The only thing I know for sure is
that the story was intended to exist. *It must be told.* This pencil
moves unconsciously, but my soul burns in the writing. In rapping
to his dead brother on "Questions," Daniel Dumile told him that
everything was going according to plan. That very instrumental
now plays in my speakers, on repeat, and my soul burns with the
knowing.

CHAPTER SIX

The bearded man, known as DJ Concise on selected week-nights, couldn't help himself. Rap fans from my generation are easy targets of nostalgia. Maneuvering deftly on his turntables amid a tangle of cords that curled around his feet like vines, he let an old Motown record play. Some of the artists, standing around holding drinks, broke off their conversation to hear where he was taking us. Something crazy was about to drop. Finally, the trigger phrase for "What We Do" came on, and general bedlam ensued. The sample echoed as Concise let the needle drop on the other record, timing it perfectly. Now Freeway was growling about crackin' 40s at sunset over that Just Blaze beat we all loved in high school. Everyone in our small circle of rap-oriented *farangs* lost their heads, the other *farangs* gave remote smiles over their drinks, and the Thais, enmeshed in their own web, glanced at us in passing interest. Such is the case with Chiang Mai hip-hop parties.

Topic 36 isn't a place you'd expect to find a hip-hop party, but then again, few places in Chiang Mai are. It's not far from the river, east of the city, where the water, once silver with moonlight, now reflects the pellucid glow of restaurants, nightclubs, and karaoke bars. Topic 36 isn't really a nightclub, though—it's more like an open, grassy courtyard, strung with lights, that could just as easily host a circus as it could a dance party. People order cocktails at a little grass hut converted into a bar. Not because that's all the locals can muster; rather, it's what the foreigners like to see. Much of Chiang Mai, actually, is a Thai interpretation of what foreigners like to see. Molded in our image, for better or for worse.

The air was heavy with liquor and cigarettes. Stray cats slinked in the shadows. Soon it would be time for a sound check. Source swaggered over to our group, showing all of his teeth. He had a red St. Louis Cardinals snapback on with a white hand towel slung over the shoulder of his black tee. This was his element. We dapped up with the standard embrace, bumping shoulders and clasping hands.

"Showtime, Prism!" He made a big show of greeting everyone, clinking glasses. Source could run for town council if he wanted, I swear.

As usual, it was a remarkably random group of people. There was an interracial couple from South Africa, a feisty Thai-American bar owner, a soft-spoken bass player and his traveling cousin, a Chinese copywriter from London, and Eric B, a goateed bachelor always on the hunt for an exotic tryst. There was also this tall guy named Craig who seemed to know me quite well, but about whom I struggled to remember anything substantial. I had told Hop to come out for the show. Whether or not he would make it was anyone's guess.

Source, meanwhile, had thrown himself into an animated explanation of taking his kids to a rock-climbing park, waving his free arm in big circles to indicate losing his balance. He accidentally collided with the bass player's cousin mid-swing, sending his drink crashing to the ground. The guy threw his hands up in frustration.

"*Shit*, my bad, bro! I'm such a klutz...here, what are you

drinking? I'll go buy you another one."

"Yeah, Jack Daniel's on the rocks," the guy replied coldly, still holding his hands out to either side in a victimized fashion.

"Really sorry about that, man, just gimme a sec. Slice of lime?"

"Sure."

Concise and I happened to exchange an ironic glance. Earlier, we had heard this guy go on about all the reasons Chiang Mai was a backwards, undeveloped place. Claiming to have worked for some NGOs in Ghana, he was obsessed with the idea of "development," chronically unsatisfied with any country that didn't resemble Singapore in soullessness. Having sustained a motorbike accident after arriving, his right knee and elbow were bandaged. His worst suspicions about the kingdom, it seemed, had been confirmed.

"I might just go back to the hotel," the grouch said loudly to his host—who looked terribly uncomfortable in a way bass players never should.

There was a silence. Most of us were too "chill" to know how to manage the situation.

"Well, this is fuckin' awkward," blurted Martin, the Thai-American bar owner. He always talked a little fast. "Let me tell you guys about this situation with my favorite Korean restaurant, it's crazy, just—"

"No one cares about your favorite Korean restaurant," laughed Eric B, stroking his chin.

"Go to hell! No, I'm serious. Just listen, okay? There's not even any girls here to look at yet, you maniac. So I go to this Korean place every week in Santitam, right? The best kimchi in the country, no joke. It's this Korean immigrant couple that runs it—yo, Concise, that speaker is fucked! Someone help him, please—anyways, I go there one night a couple weeks ago like usual. I notice the guy isn't there. 'What the hell,' I'm thinking, 'he's always there.' Well, it turns out, the couple went and got a divorce! They broke up!"

"Don't tell everyone about your K-drama habit, Martin," teased Source, returning with the promised Jack Daniel's. The grouchy cousin accepted the glass with a nod.

"Shut up! I'm telling them about that Korean place in Santitam," Martin insisted.

"Oh, *that* shit was crazy," Source laughed. He turned to me. "Prism, we're on in ten..."

"Anyways, let me finish the story! Okay, so, I dunno, five or six days later, I go back there, right? Guess what I saw!" He slapped an inattentive Craig on the shoulder, whose gaze was fixed on a pair of Euro girls walking to the bar. "Dude, it's 11:30 a.m., there's some HAIRY foreign dude, *shirtless*, smoking a cigarette next to the front door. And I'm talking, like, he's *chillin'*, you know? He's comfortable. He probably spent the night there."

"And?" queried Eric B. A joint had started to mysteriously circulate in our little group; everyone was loose again, head-nodding, ready to laugh at the slightest provocation.

"Dude, let me explain something to you, okay? If you're a restaurant owner and I go to your establishment frequently, it's because it has a wholesome family atmosphere, okay? That's what customers want to see. A husband and wife, maybe a kid, fighting against all odds to have a successful business. Am I lying? You can't just get a divorce, then have all types of creeps hanging around that you're sleeping with! I'm sorry, I have standards. I say no to *one-night stand kimchi*. And you should too, Eric B!"

"*One-night stand kimchi*," we repeated, redoubling in laughter. Everyone was leaning on one another's shoulders in hilarity, trying to talk through coughing fits. Martin made his closing statements over the commotion, gesturing like an Italian, a pleased smile curling his lips. His Thai partner sidled up to him and his demeanor changed, the American persona instantly replaced with his Thai one. There's no swiftness that can compare to that of a bilingual brain as it switches from one OS to another.

"...and it doesn't even seem like anyone cares, don't they know this town contains a UNESCO heritage site?" Everyone's ears perked up as laughter subsided. "Chiang Mai has so much potential but it's all being wasted, in my opinion. Look at these power lines, for example. This should be in violation of the country's safety protocols! And what, people just go about, caught in their super-stition of lottery numbers and what-not?..."

The acidic chatter of the grouch again filled our ears. He had corralled the wayward Craig, who seemed to be only half-listening. There was an indecisive moment where each of us, fighting social uneasiness, tried to determine whether we should address the grouch's statements or let it blow over and steer conversation in a new direction. The messy result was that Source turned to me and asked if I was ready for a mic-check at the same time the Chinese girl from London openly challenged the grouch's logic, accusing him of "paternalistic thinking."

Walking toward the stage, I found myself repeating his words. *The superstition of lottery numbers.* I thought about how fictional my experiences with Nim would sound to someone like that. My im-age as a white rapper probably wouldn't help my case, either. I cracked a smile and searched for Nim in the crowd. There weren't too many people—probably less than fifty. Here they were, ready to hear some rap music in Chiang Mai, Nepalese yoga pants and all. I sometimes looked into the eyes of audience members as they watched me emote over kicks and snares, their pupils flickering with the spectacle; each of them looked, I thought, to be on the verge of confiding a secret, something they had hidden from public censure, maybe even from themselves—as though my amplified confessions tempted their own. They, too, had probably seen reality confirm superstition at some point or another. Maybe reality was the superstition we were all waiting to be proven false.

I spotted Nim and waved at her. She was sitting at the bar with a tall cocktail in her hand, chatting with the girl serving drinks. Her cheeks were already flushed in intoxication. I said her name into the mic and asked if she was drunk. Nim, surprised, shook her fist at me—and almost fell off the stool. *Classic.* I was in the middle of the sound check when Concise called me over. He had his equipment set up on a table beneath a tent next to the stage.

"Be honest, you vibin'?"

"If it weren't for the haters."

Concise snickered, his trance of purposeful head-nodding unbroken. He was a dark-skinned guy with dreads from Indiana. I liked him because he always kept things simple. Concise let his music do the talking. Otherwise, he was quiet around people, content to observe them while keeping interactions to a minimum. You had to win his trust for him to speak more than three sentences to you. It was almost like the wheels-of-steel gave Concise an excuse not to enter unwanted conversations. There was a silence between us; De La Soul's "Stakes Is High" filled the speakers.

"When Source bumped into ol' dude, I had already seen that whole situation occurring."

"Yeah?"

"Accidents aren't always accidental. Sometimes we do it to ourselves. Just through our actions and our whole energy. Look at him: bandaged up, shirt splattered with cheap whiskey, or whatever it was. That's on *him*."

I couldn't think of anything to say, but it made a lot of sense to me.

"So y'all are jumping on some Quik tonight, huh?"

"Yeah, it's about time we try something different. You like that 'Rosecrans' track?"

"It's cool. Quik is a *monster*. Took forever for me to track down this instrumental, but it came through for y'all. Are we looping the eight-bar verse section, letting it ride, or what?"

"Good question," I laughed. "We need our own Quik-type beat soon."

"You 'type-beat' ass rappers," he shot back with a grin. "You're not answering me, though, Prism."

"We can let it ride," I said finally.

Concise nodded. Source was beginning to make his opening overtures to the crowd, letting them know it was *on*. I clapped our DJ on the shoulder and ascended the stage. The beat switched, our mics were hot, and the world was ours. I always started my performances with that AZ verse from *Illmatic*. The multi-syllable cadence rides most mid-tempo beats perfectly. Its complexity makes it easier to spit, if that makes any sense. More than anything, though, it lets me pull the crowd into *my* sphere of hip-hop, the stuff I grew up with.

I get comfortable in the space of my PA-projected voice and just flow. At this point, the audience knows exactly what they're getting: *lyricism*. They lean in closer, trying to catch my message. Now I'm on cruise control.

Time passes differently on stage because there isn't a sense of duration. The whole time we're up there, it's like one moment, ever-expanding and uninterrupted. That's why I believe that at the zenith of human accomplishment, there is no effort—only focus. (I promise I didn't take that from Thích Nhất Hạnh.) That's also why I love spitting with Source. He never forgets about the crowd. While I'm up there laser-beaming rhymes like a robot, he brings in the call-and-response. When he says C-N, they say X, etc. The energy is tremendous, but it's over in the blink of an eye.

Tonight, however, we *would* be interrupted. By what, exactly, it's hard to say. We had reached the Quik instrumental, the halfway point of our set. Concise eased the beat in effortlessly. Source rapped about Chiang Mai, then I started to do the same. Everything was smooth. Eric B had even slipped his arm around some young girl and started whispering in her ear.

Suddenly, though, the spell was broken. Everyone started looking to the right of the stage, toward the Topic 36 entrance from the road. Still rapping, I cut my eyes in that direction. An old green Volkswagen van was charging through the gate, causing an uproar. A black dog, hanging out of the passenger window, barked aggressively.

Where did I know this van from?

It screeched to a halt, then surged forward again. At that moment, I understood everything. It was *Hop*. A very drunk Hop, at that. I saw the grouch dive into some weeds along the fence to avoid getting hit. Concise's words repeated in my head—*we do it to ourselves*—and that was the last part of reality that I recognized for several minutes.

Right then, everything stopped. Someone hit the pause button on Topic 36. There was no yelling, no movement, no action. I suddenly felt like I was in a wax museum. Each person was frozen in their position, inert.

A folding chair, barreled by Hop's front fender, stood suspended at a forty-five-degree angle in the air. The dog's mouth gaped open viciously.

I looked at Source, next to me on stage—his eyes were wide, and his dismay at Hop's entrance had sent him into a squat, his right hand stretched into a "stop" signal. I was still holding the mic in my right hand, but I found it immovable. I let go and it just hung there. There was only one sound: the opening synth progression of the Quik instrumental, stuck on a loop, no drums. It just kept going like that, on and on. Each person around me was like a statue, lost in a forest of statues, all cast in an expression of alarm or curiosity. I looked for Nim at the bar but didn't see her. The synths were getting eerier with each loop.

My eyes detected movement...I thought I could hear a voice. A Thai woman was making her way over to me. I gasped. It was the librarian woman, beckoning to me as she neared the stage.

I considered running but thought better of it. My memory of that odor at the French library flashed into my senses again. The statues' suspended alarm now mimicked my own. The librarian motioned at me with familiarity.

"*Pai nai ma, pai nai ma*[73]?"

I felt my breath catch in my throat. The pattern of her turtleneck was composed entirely of tiger butterflies, all fitting together like glowing puzzle pieces. She drew nearer to me still, then stopped short, examining me slowly. Her gaze met mine. One of her eyebrows arched ironically, almost disapprovingly.

"*Hen kaa kuam ti rao song bai ra blao*[74]?"

"*Kaa kuam arrai*[75]?" I got the sense that she knew what I was really asking; the question I didn't know how to ask (in any language). The librarian's eyes sparkled. A single strand of hair was pasted to her damp forehead.

Another voice interjected over the synths: it was Nim, yelling my name. I wheeled around. She was running between the statues,

---

[73] *Pai nai ma, pai nai ma:* "Where have you been?" (ไปไหนมา)

[74] *Hen kaa kuam ti rao song bai ra blao:* "Did you get the message we sent or not?" (เห็นข้อความที่เราส่งไปหรือเปล่า)

[75] *Kaa kuam arrai:* "What message?" (ข้อความอะไร)

trying to reach the stage. The librarian was slowly disappearing in front of me until all that was left of her was the tiger butterfly turtleneck, glowing so brightly that I had to shut my eyes.

Now everything around me started to fast-forward, as a lagging video does when the lost connection is restored. The lights cut out, the stage faded away, and people's voices reached my ears again.

I took a moment to get my bearings. I was still at Topic 36, but the stage was now empty: I was on my butt, hands in the dirt. I looked up. Everything was dark. All of the attention was still on Hop and his crazy green van, which had come to a stop. People weren't statues anymore—drunk, they had partly regained their power of movement. I could sense someone next to me on the ground. Naturally, it was Nim. Her figure bolted abruptly into an upright position.

"SUPHANKANLAYA! SUPHANKANLAYA!"

Nim's voice was shrill, a voice not entirely her own. It scared the hell out of me. I put an arm around her and she melted into my chest, whimpering. *"Hai chan klab ban,*[76] *Prism, glua kun pai*[77]*, hai chan klab ban…"*

Outlines of tiger butterflies still flickered in my vision, dancing across the darkness. I felt a hand on my shoulder.

"Yo Prism, you guys good?" Concise.

"Bah[78]*,"* I said to Nim, pulling myself up.

Thai and English voices mingled in confusion around us. Nim clung to my shoulder.

"Prism," our DJ said, drawing closer and eyeing Nim with concern, "what type of shit have you gotten into, man? I saw what

---

[76] *Hai chan klab ban:* "Take me home" (ให้ฉันกลับบ้าน)

[77] *Prism, glua kun pai:* "This is too scary" (กลัวเกินไป)

[78] *Bah:* "Come on" (ปะ)

happened—" Concise broke off, looking upward with squinted eyes. The lights were back on. An ironic cheer went up from the patrons of Topic 36. I spotted Eric B and his Thai mistress making out close to the entrance, oblivious. About ten feet away, Hop was extracting himself from his van, a stubborn look on his face, one arm raised in drunken defiance.

"*Aow Chang, kuwad yai[79]. Raew[80]!*"

He staggered as if to reach the bar, one arm waving in the air, but instead he fell into the arms of Topic 36 staff members, who carefully dragged him over to a table and sat him down.

Hop collapsed in a fit of glorious laughter. The grouch approached, attempting to charge Hop with his sins. The Thais brushed him away like a fly buzzing at their ears.

I heard that when the grouch called the police that night, the party continued, with the only result being that Hop unknowingly paid for several rounds of the bar's finest whiskey.

Meanwhile, I had to get Nim home. Concise dapped me up, still concerned, and I told him I'd call him later. I was dying to know what he meant by "I saw what happened."

What could he possibly have seen? I wondered.

Source spotted me as I escorted Nim out to the blue Yamaha. I pointed at Nim and inclined my head, knowing that he would assume she was on the verge of blacking out from cocktails. He threw me a peace sign. I blinked my eyes as I climbed onto the bike; my retina was still swimming with butterflies.

Nim slumped her head onto my shoulder and we rode off, the sound of my motor mixing with the screech of a metal partition being pulled down at a nearby shop front.

---

[79] *Aow Chang, kuwad yai:* "I'll have a big bottle of Chang beer." (เอาช้างขวดใหญ่)

[80] *Raew:* "Hurry up!" (เร็ว)

All of this was more or less how Nim determined, with confidence, that she was a reincarnation of King Naresuan's legendary sister—hardly an answer in itself.

FORM C

S. didn't make the same mistake as my captors. She knew exactly how to win my trust: with good food, and lots of it. The second time she came to my room, my stomach was growling terribly. Buad tang mak[81]. *I didn't tell her, but she knew. She asked me if I was hungry. Of course I was.* "Du menu gan, kha[82]," *she smiled. I looked at her, confused. Not here, S. told me, somewhere else on the military base. I would know when I found it. She sat down and nodded at me with glittering eyes. That was the first time I giggled since coming to Nakhon Phanom. Closing my eyes, I located the menu in seconds. The menu was yellow with pink lettering, sitting on the top of a filing cabinet, smeared on the top left corner with some kind of sauce. I didn't need to read it for long.* "Moo ka ta! Moo ka ta[83]!" *It was the tastiest meal I ever had. My mouth still waters thinking about it, the tender slices dripping in* nam chim suki[84], *still hot from the grill.* Kod arroi[85]. *After that, S. always brought me any dish I wanted. It was from a special restaurant for the five-star generals on base. Little did they know that their Wonder Woman slave was eating as good*

---

[81] *Buad tang mak:* Stomach pain (ปวดท้อง)

[82] *Du menu gan, kha:* "Check the menu." (ดูเมนูกัน)

[83] *Moo ka ta:* "Barbecue pork!" (หมูกระทะ)

[84] *Nam chim suki:* Suki sauce (น้ำจิ้มสุกี้)

[85] *Kod arroi:* "Fucking delicious!" (โคตรอร่อย)

as they were. My friendship with S. did two things. It made me feel like a daughter again, and it made me hate the military men with a passion. I could barely hide my resentment when I saw them. Maybe that was my mistake. Under her guidance, I discovered dignity and pride. S. was a serious woman. She was very intelligent, but she also had a generous spirit. My child instincts helped me read the kindness in her harsh mannerisms. S. didn't tell me who she was right away. She knew that I wouldn't have believed her. The first time she visited, she didn't even explain the roses. I asked them what they were for. "Dok gulab mai dai me wai puah hi kid, me wai puah hi dom glin tao nan[86]," she said, pushing a red bud to my nose. I looked at her with suspicion. She didn't seem to want anything from me, but how could I know? I had a dim understanding that I was in the middle of something I could never understand. Even now...chang meng[87]! I took the rose from her and let the fragrance fill my nostrils. She asked me what the military men made me do, and I told her. The only thing, S. replied, was to do as I was told for now, and soon she would give me more instructions. She started visiting me every couple of days, usually a few hours after the military men had brought me dinner. I would hold a rose, spinning the stem in my hands, and tell S. about my psychic travels. In reading this, you might make the mistake of thinking that to be a beautiful image. If you knew the fear that covered my little heart like a shadow, you would think differently. One day, I had just finished another special meal of moo ka ta. *I was talking, spinning the rose in my hand, when one of the thorns pricked my finger. I yanked my hand away, then looked down. Blood was trickling from the wound and, for some reason, I thought of* Mae, *how she would make a fuss about it. I looked at S. and started crying. She peered into my eyes without any expression. Had I made a mistake? That was when I felt the old feeling: I was moving off my chair, slowly floating up toward the ceiling.*

---

[86] *Dok gulab mai dai me wai puah hi kid, me wai puah hi dom glin tao nan:* "Roses aren't for thinking, only smelling." (ดอกกุหลาบไม่ได้มีไว้เพื่อให้คิด มีไว้เพื่อให้ดมกลิ่นเท่านั้น)

[87] *Chang meng:* "Forget it!" (ช่างแม่ง)

I looked down at S. Her face was fierce, fierce like the face of a monk in concentration. Her lips never moved but I could hear her voice in my head, fuzzy at first, like a radio with bad reception...when it came into focus, I felt a shock running through my arms and legs. I started seeing pictures flashing through my head, pictures of San Kampaeng, my parents, the luk ban fai *as it crashed to earth near our* muban. Did you see this...Did you see this....*I saw my playmate's face as she held onto my ankle, pulling me back to the ground, then my father as he leaned in closer to my ear...*Mukon nang hen bap nee chai mai...Mukon nang hen bap nee chai mai[88]...*I had never heard a thought in my mind that wasn't my own. It's like hearing someone speak to you in your voice. I saw again the pagoda, the incense, the flowers on Visakha Bucha day.* "Rao roo tuk yang[89]." *She realized I was overwhelmed; slowly, I came back to my chair like a falling leaf.* "Tay wa," *S. said aloud,* "rao prom hai shuay, kha[90]." *With a start, I looked down at my finger. The wound was gone. I tasted the skin at the tip of my finger. No blood. I looked at her with my eyes rounder than temple gongs. She laughed. I had been exposed to a frequency of hyperspace when the* luk ban fai *crashed, she told me. That's why they were interested in me. I pretended to know what she meant. And what about her, I wondered?* "Pua kao kid wa chan ben sai lop kong satan tud farang say[91]." *When she said things like that, she would look at me sharply, a clear sign that I was receiving a secret I couldn't appreciate. S. used the English word* "spaceship" *to describe the image that still echoed in my mind. I never heard her talk about aliens or other planets...only timelines. There is no timeline, she said, that doesn't have an infinity of outcomes, nor is there a timeline whose outcomes aren't changeable. Our*

---

88 *Mukon nang hen bap nee chai mai...Mukon nang hen bap nee chai mai:* "You saw something like this, right?" (เมื่อก่อนน้องเห็นแบบนี้ใช่ไหม)

89 *Rao roo tuk yang:* "We know everything." (เรารู้ทุกอย่าง)

90 *Rao prom hai shuay, kha:* "But we are here to help." (แต่เราพร้อมให้ช่วย)

91 *Pua kao kid wa chan ben sai lop kong satan tud farang say:* "They think I'm a spy at the French embassy." (พวกเขาคิดว่าฉันเป็นสายลับของสถานทูตฝรั่งเศส)

timeline had, in its future, created a Planet Earth of automatons that threat-ened the security of people around this darajak[92]. *To change the result, some of them had banded together to rehabilitate the timeline by being reborn as hu-mans in the pre-robot era. This is the time of our current lives, according to what S. told me. The problem was that most of these beings, once they were born into this part of the timeline as humans, couldn't remember that they were something more than human. She called these people* chang puak[93]. *In Thai, there are many things we call* chang puak. *Often, it's used for something that has its own special uniqueness.* Pa *used that word to point out the Milky Way on nights we could see all the stars. S. told me that the amnesia of the* chang puak *was the biggest challenge in stopping the "Archonites." That was the second non-Thai word she used that day. According to her, the Archonites were timeline parasites. They caused people to imprison themselves in their own tech-nology. They used politicians, prime ministers, and powerful organizations to confuse normal people. That was why we were here now. As more* chang puak *became awakened, our numbers would grow, and this timeline would be reha-bilitated.* "Me klin hom mak, chai mai luk[94]," *S. asked me, tilting her head at the roses on the table. I am writing these stories at my own peril. Many times, I've asked myself if it's worth the risk, although I couldn't even define the risk if you asked me. I simply know that if my memories are true, then there is someone who should know what I know. It could change everything for them. That would make my life mean something more than it does now, putting on these different masks, living in fear, talking without breaking my silence. I can't tell if I'm asleep or awake anymore. S. told me that every* chang puak *born into this part of the world had chosen, before they were human, to be awakened to their mission by buying a single rose from a flower merchant at 11 p.m. under a half-moon. It didn't always work, though. Sometimes they*

---

[92] Darajak: Galaxy (ดาราจักร)

[93] *Chang puak:* White elephants (ช้างเผือก)

[94] *Me klin hom mak, chai mai luk:* "They smell nice don't they, child?" (มีกลิ่นหอมมากใช่ไหมลูก)

only got visions, weird thoughts, dreams they kept forgetting. They needed a Wonder Woman, S. laughed. She would describe a few flower merchants in Chiang Mai, the ones wandering in the old city at night, and I could use them as "targets" to find some of the sleeping chang puak. *I could help S. and her friends change the timeline, if I wanted to. Then maybe I could even go home again. I just needed to find a few white elephants with red roses, that was all.*

CHAPTER SEVEN

There is no dreamer who doesn't constantly doubt his dreams, however eagerly he may report them to a friend or stranger. The question of whether or not they're real leads him to bouts of brooding in public places, which itself has more practical consequences, such as forgetting a wallet at a laundromat or failing to respond with immediacy to a girlfriend's distraught text. These minor situations being eventually resolved, he finds himself circling back around to the original question, shining with forbidden radiance in a secret part of his mind. A friend calls for a favor but, much to their dismay, becomes held up for over half an hour. The dreamer waves off their request with annoyance, as if his kindness is a foregone conclusion. He describes the dream in painstaking detail, losing himself, not noticing the urgency of his friend's "mm-hm's." The dreamer only desires to banish that doubt, which otherwise threatens to overshadow the magic of the dream. His mistake is in assuming that the most recent dream was his last glance at a world he'd never seen before, which itself is (probably) a mistaken thought.

In my case, of course, dreams and waking life could no longer be told apart. This only had the effect of multiplying my doubts, in a way. The reader might recall my friend at the funeral home nauseated by my "positivity." But that very positivity, the big smiles and hopeful remarks, was in fact just the flip-side of the oppressive doubt that overshadowed my private moments. It's rather like a person whose house is next to a landfill and is thus always complimented for how his house is perfumed with air freshener. The visitor doesn't realize that his host is constantly fighting against a force that threatens to choke the air of his home with pestilence. He only knows that his friend's house always has a pleasant smell. That's how people experienced being around me, as far as I could tell.

Even for all that, however, I could also feel an anxiety of urgency building with each new lottery win, with every new glimpse at the supernatural. There is no person, at any age, who is prepared to lose their mother. It's not something you can practice for or rehearse, like a series of rhymes tethered by cadence in a song. Anytime someone loses their mother, it is the first time they have done so, and it's as sudden as a storm. Life is altered in ways one can choose to either recognize or ignore. One moment, I'm guiding her to the end of sentences with the words she couldn't find, and *then*...I simply had no preconception of what life was supposed to be like after it happened. Now someone was giving us keys to the lottery, and we didn't know why. After seeing the librarian dressed in butterflies, I could *feel* that these things were connected, even if I doubted it. My anxiety came from expecting a resolution to my grief, in allowing myself to hope that all of these events were strung together to give me an answer, a final reassurance. Was that hope not just another way to avoid the acceptance of loss, a lottery's fool's gold?

Of course, much of my story isn't fit to be believed, and even if it is, it will probably be retold in the tone of voice a person uses to say their friend thought they saw a creature in the woods. I admit that I don't always entirely believe it, either. There have been times when, staring directly into a pink Chiang Mai sunset from my veranda, I've rejected the whole story altogether, only to once again admit that there is no other explanation. For now, let me just say that I am writing as much to quiet my own doubts as I am to fulfill certain obligations.

After the stuff that happened at Topic 36, I think Nim and I were in similar moods. We left each other's messages on "read" for a long time, and when we did respond, they were normally curt answers. The truth is, we were a little scared, but neither of us wanted to show it. Instead, Nim sent me glamour shots of her coconut smoothies or frothy lattes, the photogenic kind with a rabbit face neatly traced on its surface. She was content to fill our chat with Thai *sanuk*[95]-signaling but stopped short of inviting me anywhere. (Her lottery luck still hadn't run out, apparently.) I tried to stabilize in the steady refrain of "home noises"—the clatter of pans or slam of the screen door, the creaking of a carport's gate, the drone of the water pipes. I was in the steady orbit of coffee grinders, living for the first whiff of Lanna coffee beans in the morning, when my memory was still covered in the purple film of dreams—always mother-dreams.

I had thought of her again several nights after the Topic 36 show. I was at a specialty market in the Nimman neighborhood with a friend. We were browsing the stalls, sidestepping our way through the dinner crowd at a halting pace. I caught sight of a wide-brimmed bonnet and yellow dress on a mannequin and stopped in my tracks. The impression was too much; I wiped beads of sweat from my forehead and felt short of breath. All I could think of was

---

[95] *Sanuk:* Fun, enjoyment (สนุก)

how pretty it would look on her, how naturally it would fit her elegant style, how she would smile when she opened the gift bag in her ethereal delight. I almost bought it just *because*—but my friend hurried me on, and shortly my attention was redirected to the smoky flavor of *luk chin*[96] meatballs, which we devoured under the proud gaze of the *luk chin* lady.

Several days later, I was on my way to Source's studio for a supposed barbecue when I remembered having had that same dream again—the one with the rose-colored gift box and the fog. It came to me as a shock. I was maneuvering around splashy potholes on a lonely back road after a spell of rain. Distant mountains could be seen on the horizon, floating over the rice fields' sea of empty green, with the low flight of two egrets being the only stir of motion besides my own. The moist smell of the earth quieted my city-dwelling mind, and gradually fragments of the dream crept back into my awareness. All of it was the same: her approach, her offer, her morphing into a young girl looking up at me. Only in this case, there was something like an appendix to the dream. The little girl was leading me through a meadow, a meadow that stretched out forever in each direction, and in the tiny grasp of her hand I understood that we were going somewhere important, maybe a temple. I'd always imagined how astounding it would be to interact with my parents when they were children, if I was able to somehow jump timelines in the style of cartoons and theoretical physicists. Here, though, that kind of interpretation seemed trite. That couldn't be it.

I asked myself if this picture of my mother as a girl wasn't just another trick of the mind to distract me from the way I had last seen her, convulsing on her deathbed in morphine tremors, her

---

[96] *Luk chin:* Meatballs (ลูกชิ้น)

body like a thing unplugged. None of that had seemed real; rather, it seemed like a crude performance that had nothing to do with the principle of *her*. In that moment, truth be told, I hadn't felt anything, and no tears came. I understood that she had already made her exit, and so this entire deathbed vigil was just a formality to be endured, tolerated, understood through a host of mechanical terms in a hospice brochure. Her smile no longer inhabited that slackened mouth, and the dull blue of the eyes wasn't actually hers. It was a far cry from that brilliant, doting woman I'd known, the one who could make a yellow dress look more expensive than it was, the one whose smile was sunshine, the one whose aroma of fresh-made bread filled the air of countless summer evenings. Even this dream of my mother as a little girl, somehow, seemed much closer to the truth than the cruel sight of her expiring.

The rain momentarily resumed, and I got off the motorbike and ducked under a little wooden *sala* on the side of the road for cover.

Source's studio was really just an extra bedroom with a microphone stand and a computer monitor, flanked by rumbling speakers and scattered children's toys. The room was dark, only dimly lit with lava lamps and hazy with blunt smoke, the spotlight of the computer screen illuminating Source's face. Nike shoeboxes sat agape on a brown sofa strewn with brightly colored tees, some still with their tags on. Most producers' studios are like this, really. You expect the studio space to reflect the majesty of the music created, to be like a miniature palace with gleaming records on the wall; often, you just find someone unshaven sitting in the clutter of yesterday's *pad thai*[97] takeaway, manufacturing his own emerald cities on three hours' sleep. I could almost see the cloud of missed calls

---

[97] *Pad thai:* Popular dry noodle dish (ผัดไทย)

hanging in the air. When you find a guy like Source holed up in his room alone, not in the middle of a crowd, you can sense all the invisible hands reaching out to grab his attention. He rose to greet me.

"The man of the hour," he declaimed with a big grin, wiping a clump of ashes from his shirt. When I extended my hand, he recoiled in mock fright, raising his arms to protect himself.

"Seriously, bro?"

"You know I had to convince my wife to let you over, right?" Source pulled me into a brisk, consoling embrace. "We had to put a couple extra cans of Fanta out in front of the spirit house just to make sure the energy wasn't funky!"

"Come on."

"I'm fuckin' wit' ya," he said in a softer voice, turning back to his monitor. Today it was all-black-everything: black tee, black shorts, black snapback, with a gold cross hung around his neck. Even his loungewear was impeccable. "Did Concise get at you yet?"

"He's not coming over?"

"We took Leelawadee over to the doctor's this morning, she wasn't feeling well. Had to cancel the barbecue, we might do it next Saturday, if you're around…"

"Oh," I said, caught off guard. "Is it a bad time?"

"You're good, man, sit down," said Source, waving his hand in a gracious show of exasperation.

I shoved some shoe boxes over and took a seat on the sofa, not saying anything. Had there ever been a barbecue planned in the first place? Maybe it was just a pretense to get me in the studio. I waited for Source's explanation, watching him in profile. He was back in his seat, headphones halfway on, gazing intently at the soundboard levels in his Logic window. You have to treat producers like wizards in front of an open portal—breaking their concentration better be worth it.

"Tell me what you think of this," he said distractedly, filling the room with the thump of a naked kick-and-snare. The percussive glitter of hi-hats followed, and a composition gradually took shape. Source lit a blunt and passed it to me, his eyes still on the screen. Rather than turn the music down, he raised his voice to give an explanation.

"I took the BPM of that Quik track—'Rosecrans,' yeah?—then I switched up the snares and hats a little, you hear that?" I took two puffs and paused, analyzing the drums respectfully. Source pointed his finger in the air to get my attention. "Here come the horns, wait for it..."

I'd told myself I wasn't going to get high in the studio, but part of me was relieved for the opportunity. Maybe I needed some mental distance from Supankanlaya, Naresuan, and butterflied librarians. The pattern of the keys switched up, the kicks dropped out, and the promised horns arrived. I nodded my head. I liked it.

"That's the hook, that's the hook, and then—" The pattern resumed and the kicks returned. "Then your verse starts here, see what I'm saying?" Source reached for the blunt, satisfied. "Just a little eight-bar thing," he added vaguely.

"This thing is hard," I commented in admiration, my speech already clipped by the cannabis.

"That's what she said," Source quipped, cackling. He shot me a look. "Damn, Prism, you faded already? I need to get some vocals from you, buddy!"

"I want to switch up my verse a little bit. Gimme a sec, I got my lyrics here."

Source nodded and turned back to the monitor, stroking his chin in thought. Smoke hung around us in a haze as though we had a fog machine from the *Thriller* set. I noticed that he was carefully avoiding *the* topic, that of Topic 36. Besides the obvious reference at our greeting, it seemed as though he were sidestepping it altogether. Maybe it was because he hadn't noticed anything, but I got the sense that he had, and was choosing not to address it.

There had been a note of disapproval in his joke about the spirit house—or was that just me overthinking it? In my weed-clouded mind, the anxieties started to fractalize and redouble themselves. This is why I tried to stay away from cannabis. Every thought or observation became its own all-encompassing mandala that threatened to consume my attention (and confidence). Especially in this case. Regardless of what Source was thinking, I reasoned, the message was clear that he wanted to move forward with the Chiang Mai song. I took out my lyrics and slowly started revising, whispering rhymes under my breath.

Some time passed before I realized that Source had stripped the track down to its drums again, inserting some kind of Thai voice that echoed stridently as he tried to find the right placement. Some of the "sample debris" followed it, in this case a rash of whirling organs with peaking frequencies, like hearing snatches of a carnival on an empty street. By this I guessed Source was sampling an old record from the Molam era. He idly played with the organs before finally silencing them. The obscure voice remained, and I tried to catch it: *"Sombot, sombot."*

"What's that sample?" I queried.

"Got it off this Isaan Greatest Hits joint," Source said proudly. "Shit sounds kinda fly…"

"Do you know what she's saying?"

"No fuckin' idea, bro. Might have to call the wife in for translation services," he grinned.

"Sombot, sombot," I repeated. "Hold on, I think I can figure it

out..." I made a couple of attempts at spelling it in an online translator. Finally, the spelling was close enough to trigger a correction, and the code was cracked. "*Sombot*[98], it means 'fortune' or 'treasure,'" I announced.

"For real?" Source lifted his arms above his head and stretched into a yawn. "That's the perfect word for that Chonburi sugar-mama Prism has!" I made a face and he laughed. "Come on and give me a mic-check."

I'd aimed at perfecting the verse I had with some tweaks and corrections, only to cross out most of those tweaks and corrections so that for all the effort, I was left with more or less what I came into the studio with. I had ventured off in an ambitious direction that proved fruitless, not even necessarily connected to the song's subject matter. Half an hour of intense concentration had yielded only this:

It's funny how one pencil
scrambles timelines
I make Chronos cry
when I write rhymes
A burst in cursive
purples night skies—
Who can criticize?
I cross the T's of
what can't be seen
by the eyes

Aside from not being related to the song's topic of Chiang Mai, I rejected these lyrics for three primary reasons. First, the pattern

---

[98] *Sombot:* Fortune, treasure (สมบัติ)

of the rhyme scheme lacked novelty, being based on the generic "write rhymes," which is sort of like using the reddest red to make your painted apple as boring as possible. Second, the attractive concept of the opening line had been overextended into a series of forced lines ending in a questionable double entendre, whose meaning was too elusive to justify the wit being expended. Finally, most of those lines had been composed in the shadow of better ones I'd forgotten before I could jot them down, giving the whole thing a false glow.

With a shrug, I went over to the mic stand. Source turned the beat on, his unspoken signal for me to rehearse a few times before recording. Standing in front of the mic, I felt like Kevin Hart—too short. I felt around for a knob until the ridged surface brushed my fingers, and now the pop filter was at my level. Headphones on, notebook held up behind the mic.

"Sombot, sombot," was my initial mic-check. The resonance of my voice enfolded me like a comforter. I felt that spark as a creator for whom everything is a mirror, through which he can experience his creations infinitely, if only for a moment.

"Gimme another one," Source urged.

A streak of mischief flashed through me. "It's funny how you call yourself *Open Source* like you just *opened The Source*, I got a clean sixteen that'll get you *open, Source,* better get your thesaurus!"

I looked over at him with a grin, but it hadn't netted the result I expected. His lips spread into a tight smile and he only shook his head. "Don't tell me those demons are giving you diss rhymes, too," he muttered in a strange voice.

"Say what?"

The door opened and a head tentatively peeked in, ready to re-treat at a moment's notice. It was Source's wife. Though her real name was Sulapon, she went by the name of *Meow*, thus taking part in that universal Thai custom by which young people adopt goofy pet names to save you the trouble of saying their real ones: choice pearls kept out of reach of the grasping foreigners. She held a plate in her outstretched hands, and Source accepted with a nod of his head. Meow greeted me with an almost apologetic *sawadee kha.*

"Tama-ren, tama-ren," she pronounced carefully, indicating the contents of the plate.

"Tamarind, baby," Source corrected. "You want some, man?" His voice had regained its charismatic tone.

"*Ma-kam[99], chai mai krub?*"

"A-ho," Meow exclaimed, turning to Source. "Why you not speak Thai like Prism?"

"What are you doing, you made dinner yet?" Source asked, ignoring her question and shooting me a look.

"Nooo," she responded in an agitated tone. "Now I watch about Malila on TikTok." She laughed self-consciously, covering her mouth with her hand.

"Malila, Malila, always with this damn Malila!" Source turned to me again. "Does Nim talk about her too?"

"All the time," I said, shaking my head.

"Now it's a big scandal for Thai people," Meow explained. It was as though the room wasn't big enough to contain her embarrassment.

"Okay, Okay," Source said by way of dismissal. Relieved, she bowed out of the room and closed the door.

The sour flesh of the tamarind fruit normally isn't my favorite, but it fulfilled the requirements of studio munchies. I got a couple takes down that evening, each recording having its pros and cons. We listened to both so many times for comparison that my ability

---

[99] *Ma-kam:* Tamarind (มะขาม)

to judge became compromised, and I left the studio that night with a dull feeling.

After Meow served us tamarinds, Concise finally called me for a video chat, delaying the recording further. I could tell that Source had been expecting the call. Concise described what he saw when Hop's van collided with the table. There was a "ripple or wave" of energy that passed through the whole space, after which I had completely dematerialized on stage—something "only Prince could do back in '86" he snickered. That was when the lights had gone out. Other people saw me disappear too, but most of them had been drinking. As Concise went on, Source seemed to grow more agitated, bouncing his right leg up and down. When Concise mentioned a friend who did energy work, Source finally interjected.

"When you take money from the djinn, you surrender your life in exchange, that's what he needs to understand. Leave the money *alone*!"

"Is that Source talking?" Concise laughed. "Tell him to chill, he's sounding way too Catholic right now."

The producer only shook his head and said no more on the topic. I gave our DJ a "concise" summary of what Nim and I had experienced with the lottery up to that point, leaving out some things here and there. The idea that I had been pulled into another dimension, experiencing a moment that didn't exist for anyone else, didn't lead me to the Faustian conclusions it had for Source. Maybe this was his weird, indirect way of staging an intervention, only Concise didn't come down as hard as he'd wanted him to. I did notice after the call, however, that Source had removed the *sombot* sample from the instrumental. I didn't bother to ask him about it.

CHAPTER EIGHT

If I am Suphankanlaya, nobody can know that," said Nim, discreetly raising a bottle of herbal ointment to her nose.

"Why not?"

"Prism, I tell you already, you not remember? For Thai people, Suphankanlaya is the good-luck goddess. So if they know, everyone here will ask for my blessing, and we can't go anywhere. Crazy *sha-bing*[100]."

We had just arrived at Wat Doi Kham, "Temple of the Golden Mountain." It might be the most popular Chiang Mai temple among locals, not just for the mountaintop views, but because its Buddha images are known for granting good fortune like cups of water.

The soaring spires of the pagoda now appeared in our view, and little children with ice cream cones darted after slouching temple dogs. We were walking past the feet of a gigantic Buddha. The story was that the giants themselves had chosen this spot, but seeing this Buddha reminded me of the kind of over-the-top prop you'd see in an old Cash Money Millionaires video.

---

[100] *Sha-bing:* Slang term used to emphasize an adjective. (ขิบเป้ง)

Wat Doi Kham was the seat of fortune, and here the road to fortune was paved with garlands of jasmine flowers sold for fifty *baht* under vendor tents. Buy a garland or two on your way, snag three incense sticks, pray at the altar, and then soon you'd be rich, maybe find a lover—or both. The winding road to the temple spiraled upward like the coils of a serpent, through the treetops. Some chose to take the staircase of a thousand steps up the other side, reasoning that fortune was better acquired through an exchange of vital energy.

"Okay," I said, nudging Nim's shoulder, "tell me about her again. She was Naresuan's sister, and…?"

Nim had been in a sour mood since the moment she fished out a fly from her *tom kha*[101] bowl at lunch. I sensed an opening to peel back her sullenness.

"Oii, Prism! Okay, I can explain to you again. In that time, the Thai princess was given to kings in Burma, for sign of loyalty—*koh jai mai*[102]? They take her there with her brothers, not *Phra*[103] Naresuan. She was pregnant, but then *Phra* Naresuan won the fight with son of Burma king. This is the famous fight in Thai history, *chai mai*. But Suphankanlaya was still in Burma with the king, and he take revenge…kill her, na."

"Before she had the baby?"

"*Chai kha*, she eight months pregnant."

"Damn."

"Prism, you can't say like that at the temple, na." She slapped my shoulder in gentle reproach.

The sound of tinkling bells carried on the air with the smell of

---

[101] *Tom kha:* Coconut-based curry soup. (ต้มข่า)

[102] *Koh jai mai:* "Do you understand?" (เข้าใจไหม)

[103] *Phra:* Title for a king. (พระ)

jasmine, the garlands of which were crowded at one particular altar like hundreds of wedding cakes, under a threshold draped in burgundy silk. We were crossing into a kind of squared pavilion at the heart of the complex. At the center was the golden *chedi*[104] that housed a lock of the Buddha's hair, and then several *viharns*[105] with their sloping roofs and curving eaves. Around the perimeter of the square were old relics, giant gongs, deities in tiger-stripe tunics, a menagerie of Buddhas. Young and old alike paraded around the *chedi*, incense sticks or yellow candles clutched in their palms. The atmosphere was that of a dazzling country fair whose implications extend beyond the day of the country fair itself.

"So if Naresuan hadn't killed the son of the Burmese king, then his sister would have lived. Right?"

"Hmm," said Nim, bowing to a bald-headed monk brushing past us. "It looks like a sacrifice. For us, we think that Suphankanlaya died so Thai people can get freedom again, for the *independence*. *Phra* Naresuan is the hero, but it was also bad for his karma, you know?"

"Crazy. And if you're Suphankanlaya, then the lottery guy is...Naresuan?"

"*Chai kha.* I'm his sister, and now he has to make merit by giving me the lottery numbers. *Hen mai*[106]? If he wants to become *nippan*[107], first he has to clear his past. Today, the monks will—" Nim searched for the words in English, teetering at an abyss. "*Phra ja attibai noi*[108]," she concluded finally, surrendering to her native tongue with an air of apology.

---

[104] *Chedi:* Pagoda (เจดีย์)

[105] *Viharns:* Building of worship (วิหาร)

[106] *Hen mai:* "Do you see?" (เห็นไหม)

[107] *Nippan:* Nirvana (นิพพาน)

[108] *Phra ja attibai noi:* The monk will explain. (พระจะอธิบายน้อย)

"Nim *krub*," I said, pulling her to the side as others walked by us, "you're my girlfriend. Are you telling me you're actually a Burmese queen from four hundred years ago?" I repeated the message in Thai, never trusting the floating dandelions of English words to find their mark.

"Yes," she replied after a moment, "that is what I tell you. You believe me?" Nim craned her head to one side, searching my face.

"Maybe," I grinned. "But where does this leave me? If you're Naresuan's sister, does that mean I'm the old king of Burma?"

"*Mai chai*, Prism," she sighed, shaking loose of my hand and resuming her trot in contempt. Nim had taken the question for a joke, and it *did* sound like one of my jokes, but I was more or less serious—or at least as serious as Nim was asking me to be. I felt somewhat annoyed by the caprice of her self-resolve. She was acting as though her status as a "good-luck goddess" was a foregone conclusion. I could feel this idea settling comfortably into her brain.

There was, of course, an erotic appeal to this ascension on her part, some of the possibilities of which we had already explored in the half-light of dawn. That was when our eyes were still dewy with dreams. Now, in the full light of day, the story seemed like a cheap product of merit-making Buddhism, meaningless outside our temple of sexuality.

I took a moment to look at the people around us, with their flowers and incense and meek demeanor. They were all looking for what Nim had already received, and they were most likely willing to give up far more than what they were being asked to in order to get it.

What if they knew Suphankanlaya herself was here at Wat Doi Kam, floating in their midst?

"*Diew diew*[109], let me ask you something," I said, drawing up next to her again.

"*Mai son jai*[110]," Nim huffed.

"No, listen! I just want to know if you have any memories of being Naresuan's sister. Do you remember something from that lifetime? Anything?"

We strolled through a doorway that led us out of the main square onto an open terrace that admitted a wide-lens view of the entire valley, with the settlement of Chiang Mai shimmering like a mirage off to one side, semi-veiled in a curtain of car exhaust. A reclining Buddha gazed at us from a position of vast leisure. My eyes settled on the long staircase, its balustrades two serpent tails that undulated downward like a pair of water slides into the mass of tangled green.

Nim stopped and leaned over a rail. "No, maybe I never had memories like that. But you know about the relationship with my mother, right? I ever told you about that before. When she desert me, I had a feeling like...*I don't care.* Yes, and you know why? Because I felt like I had more power than her. Even I was just nine-year-old girl. So young. At school, everyone followed me *duay*[111]. You know, Prism, I never had to get my lunch at school canteen, not even one time?"

"What do you mean?"

"Someone always bring it to me."

"*Tum mai?* You mean some boys who liked you?"

"No, everyone! I just sit and then food arrives—Nim *tam sabai sabai*[112]." She giggled, shaking her head in fond wonder.

---

[109] *Diew diew:* "Hold on." (เดี๋ยวๆ)

[110] *Mai son jai:* "I don't care." (ไม่สนใจ)

[111] *Duay:* Too (ด้วย)

[112] *Tam sabai sabai:* "I took it easy." (ทำสบายๆ)

A noise behind us made us turn around. Five saffron-orange robes rippled silently in the mountaintop breeze, their owners waiting for Nim to accompany them into the *viharn*. None of the monks made eye contact with me. Nim had told me they would take her through a ceremony, sprinkle drops of water on her head, then give her some advice on the situation.

I'm clearly just an accessory in this drama, I thought to myself, watching her depart with the stoic group. Things hadn't quite come into focus for me yet. The monks were spiritual leaders of the Thai community, that much I understood. They were looked upon as beings who stood at the nebulous borders between the everyday world and the unseen. It seemed natural that Nim would seek their counsel at this time—it was just the right *Thai* thing to do. The temple's connection to the lottery itself, though, was more vague and impalpable than I could have realized. I doubt that such a thing has ever come to the attention of many foreigners...

I was alone now. The sun emerged from behind the clouds, and I shifted uncomfortably in the heat. The bells tinkled on a fresh breeze and people milled around me, pointing at one place or another, laughing as they attempted to spot familiar things in the city from our bird's-eye view. Mountaintops always remind humans of how hopelessly small we are, how silly it is to think we're in control of the colossal domain we find ourselves in. These thoughts lighten people up, somehow.

I felt drowsy and strolled to a place in the shade where I could watch people. A strike of the gong occasionally vibrated through the scene. My thoughts turned again to Nim and her lottery prowess. She had won a fourth and a fifth time, and I had long since ceased being surprised. There was, instead, a feeling that she could never lose, that the faceless lotto man would never *let* her lose. The luck of Nim's numbers was a certainty, and I was prepared to finally surrender to its logic—only there was a part of me that was afraid of who I would become if I did. What if luck was a curse? Were all these people not slaves to the lottery?

The fourth time she won big money, there was no lotto man, only a shot-in-the-dark guess worth another 56,000 *baht*. (Dumb luck!) The fifth time, Nim again had a dream. She was a spectator among many others crowded around a soccer field. The crowd parted in front of her, and she saw a man in a red jersey crouching on the sideline, his back to her. There was a three-digit number on the back of his jersey. *718*. Those oddly placed numbers had unlocked another 66,000 *baht*. She had told me that it wasn't obvious the man in the red jersey was her lotto man, but after she woke up, she could immediately *feel* that it had been, and she bought her ticket that day with the utmost confidence. Unlike the Powerball in America, the tax Nim had to pay on these winnings was negligible.

Two strange figures appearing on the staircase captured my attention. I first saw a pair of identical heads, and as they mounted the final stairs, their full bodies came into view. There wasn't a detail of one that differed from the other; everything about them was completely identical. I watched them with curiosity. My first thought was that, whoever these tourists were, they were quite poorly dressed for a hot day in Chiang Mai, clad in all-black as they were. They each wore slacks, a sports coat, and dress shoes, accented by a tidy gold chain on the outside of the collar.

They must be regretting that wardrobe choice, I thought to myself.

They seemed to be twins, doubly oblivious to Thai climate conditions. Each had the same pencil-thin mustache, dark, slicked-back hair, and morbidly pale skin. Their features were hard to place, but they almost looked Sicilian if not for the complete absence of pigmentation. The strangest thing about these twins, however, was the way they moved. They walked stiffly, as if they didn't completely trust their legs to work, as if they were only familiar with their bodies on a theoretical level. Concise would probably use the word "suspect" to describe them.

I watched as they ambled in my direction. They were deep in conversation. One spoke more than the other as though he were a superior.

As they got closer, I noticed their eyes were bigger than normal, showing a queer gleam. I looked around to see how the Thais were reacting. Most of them seemed to ignore the strange characters, but some took pictures from a distance. This attitude confused me. Were these twins regulars at Wat Doi Kham, maybe a pair of eccentric expats who lived in the area?

Their presence was permitted but not unnoticed. The pair stopped at a spot near where I was sitting on the bench. Despite their full-black garb, they made no attempt to get out of the sun. I was surprised, somehow, to hear them talking in English. Their voices lived in a higher register, and the sound pricked my ears. They seemed to have no concern for my comprehending presence. I sat there listening, gradually picking up on their conversation against the temple's tinkling bells.

"...and we've now looked at twelve Oleon stations that rearrange the secondary sequence of events in that experience of *now*, which connects the algorithm of better *nows* to theirs, as you so callously observed earlier."

"Your quips and overall manner are intolerable, but perhaps useful to your pursuit of respectability as an ambassador."

"If your poise ever caught up with your wit, you yourself would be a keeper of time and not a sniveling apprentice assigned to me."

"My patience, Master Elezon, has become compromised by a certain mistrust in your motives. You have neglected to show me the doorways that will provide access to the source of the time locks. And yet still I must submit to your authority."

"You have made no secret of your weakness, Lumanil. We are the managers of Earth timelines, but you only manage to get ahead of yourself. If you are impatient to learn, it means you are not prepared to learn what is being put in front of you. You cannot be trusted to integrate multiple timelines at once if this weakness persists."

"I am prepared to be informed of this immediate Oleon station, Master Elezon."

"And so it is. The Tibetan doorway has conducted us to another catalyzing point in the early era of the White Elephant timeline. That is the name the local operatives have developed to characterize this experience of manipulating the planetary past. Lumanil, the appropriate time has come to ask me the question."

"What is the primary event that allowed us access to this Oleon station?"

"You have done well. Fifty-eight years prior to this example of *now*, one of the scout ships of a race serving the empire became caught in Earth density. The local humans observed its termination in the jungles bordering their city. We have built numerous secondary timelines that run off this primary event. Sacred places of worship serve as nodal points of energy transduction..."

"...and the polarities of human energy are mobilized through an ancient lottery system—you underestimate my all-term memory, Master Elezon."

"In the language of this lottery system, your statement is only a lucky guess."

"I don't need luck to meet the best of probabilities. You insult me by imputing my knowledge to base human principles."

"Luck is an instrument of reinventing the past, Lumanil.

Because the humans of these spacetime coordinates bear an especial reverence for luck, their receptivity toward the time keepers and spirit guides is expanded, and thus we can act through their consciousness to accelerate evolutionary events."

"Luck is a currency of purpose."

"You have spoken correctly. The national lottery of this kingdom has been consecrated as a galactic sorting house in which humans are selected to fulfill different missions. Their selection by one number or another was predetermined at their birth and depends on what experiences attract their consciousness."

"Here I observe a unique reverence among the humans for the station's lottery coordinators."

"They experience them as holy men blessed with magical powers, and perceive these holy men's mastery of numbers as something merely incidental to their position as priests. Although they are devotees of both the temple and the lottery, they fail to understand that it is all one institution, existing everywhere, guiding them to recreate their reality."

"This lottery hasn't escaped the influence of the empire, Master Elezon."

"The duality of their existence also exists on this timeline, and there are those humans here who will draw their numbers and serve the purpose of the empire, instead of that of the White Elephants."

"Then you hardly need me to point out that this lottery is corrupted."

"There is no lottery that isn't, Lumanil. All lotteries are necessarily corrupted with negative outcomes. We are building a parallel timeline to correct a bias of our universe toward one polarity, and so we must harness human potential through what they perceive as a game of chance. In playing this game, we accept the play of duality—something from which *you* would never excuse your-self..."

The two figures moved off, disappearing in the entrance to the pagoda's square. I rushed to the doorway to catch another glimpse of them. Somehow, it was too late; amid the jasmine carousel of worshippers, they had already slipped away, and I only spied a black pair of slacks retreating around the pagoda. There were too many people between me and the other end of the square to try and pursue them. Another strike of the gong reverberated through the scene. I could still hear the outlines of the twins' shrill voices in the air, but they were gone. I knew they weren't human, which made their awkward movements and bickering more amusing. Why they chose to look like a pair of Italian bodyguards was anyone's guess.

Most of what they said had been incomprehensible, but their remarks about the temple and lottery being one and the same had resonated with my sense that the monks here were fulfilling some kind of administrative function. They were more than just aloof cheerleaders in people's pursuit of fortune; their blessed hands held loaded dice. *Luck is an instrument of reinventing the past.* If luck could be defined in such an odd way, I wondered somewhat self-ishly why I hadn't been included in much of the "reinventing" thus far. Parallel universes always carry the distinction of being luck-ier—*other* ones, that is.

A hand on my neck sent me into a momentary panic.

"Prism," a radiant Nim giggled. "*Glua arrai kha*[113]?"

"Nothing," I snapped, frowning. "What did the monks say?"

"Babe, we have to go to immigration, na," Nim declared, taking me by the arm. "Someone important there."

---

[113] *Glua arrai kha:* "What are you afraid of?" (กลัวอะไรคะ)

"Immigration?! My visa doesn't expire for another two months…"

She let forth one of her sarcastic laughs and kissed me on the cheek. "*Mai tong brien wee-sa*[114], Prism *kha. Ja bpai kwee kab khon hoi duay kan kha*[115]."

"A lottery person at immigration? I don't get it."

"*Kuh karachakan ni*[116] immigration. See? The monk gave me, na." She handed me a card with Thai writing and the government insignia printed in the corner.

"Who is Jeerawan Ratcharot?" I asked, squinting at the formal font of the characters.

"Nim *bok laew*[117]! Government officer, she has information for us about lottery."

She was completely transformed—her face was shining with almost drunken pleasure, and I even wondered if she was intoxicated. I assumed that I was failing to understand the significance of the appointment, which confused me more.

They fail to understand it is one institution…

We were almost back to my motorbike, which was parked in the shade of a tree whose blossoms made a crimson carpet on the pavement. Nim suddenly threw herself in front of me, a wild look in her eye. Her hands ran through my hair and her pelvis pressed warmly against mine. She brought her face close, and our breath mingled deeply enough to be a prelude.

"The appointment is tomorrow, not today," she whispered.

---

[114] *Mai tong brien wee-sa:* "You don't need to change your visa." (ไม่ต้องเปลี่ยนวีซ่า)

[115] *Ja bpai kwee kab khon hoi duay kan kha:* "We'll go talk with a lottery person together." (จะไปคุยกับคนหวยด้วยกันคะ)

[116] *Kuh karachakan ni:* "It's a government officer at…" (คือข้าราชการใน)

[117] *Bok laew:* "(I) told you already!" (บอกแล้ว)

"Do you love me?"

"Nim, I—"

"Shhh!" She put a finger to my lips. "Queens get what they *want*, you know…"

I felt my blood running hot as my hands found her waist. This assault left me defenseless. There was something almost primal in the way her body clung to mine, and for a second I fancied that our passion was invincible, but then an image just past the roundness of her shoulder caught my eye, and my heart stopped.

"What is it, Prism?"

I had to do a double-take. Draped across the handlebars of my bike was a familiar black sports coat, several red petals resting in its folds. Whether it was Lumanil's or Master Elezon's, I couldn't say. When I lifted the black coat up by an index finger, it promptly evaporated, leaving the petals spinning in the air like mating butterflies.

FORM D

When I wasn't dreaming of roses, I was spying on the people purchasing them. S. sat there next to me with her hair pulled back in a tight bun. She was patient and never prodded me too much. She wasn't like P Tom. S. gave me the coordinates and let me do the rest. Night after night, I followed the khon kai gu lab[118] *through the Chiang Mai streets. They were always short old ladies, haunting the shadows of a street diner with a bundle of roses in their arms, smiling toothlessly. Everyone knew the rose ladies well enough to ignore them...unless they needed a gift for their lover, or maybe they were a* farang *tourist wandering around the moat with nothing better to do than smell flowers and watch the canals mirror the moon. I saw this all the time. I followed the rose ladies around the moat, through the old city's fortress walls, past the markets of Chiang Puak on the north side, all the way to the markets of the fortress' southern gate. "It's the night of someone's awakening," S. would remind me on evenings of a half-moon, handing me a rose. Many times, the Thai military men seemed to suspect me of something but said nothing. I was serving them well, as S. had instructed. P Tom had taken a liking to me, too. The information I provided was the most accurate of all the inmates at Nakhon Phanom, I know that now. Sometimes, he rested a hand on my knee as I*

---

[118] *Khon kai gu lab:* Rose merchant (คนขายกุหลาบ)

viewed a location for his unit, sliding it up my leg ever so slowly. Other times, he would lean in close to me as he explained a document, his breath hot on my neck. I wondered if all farangs *had breath as sour as his. I was smart enough to complain that I couldn't focus on the target when P Tom did those things. It was enough to make him back off, at least for a while. They almost discovered my friendship with S. one evening before she arrived for her usual visit. P Tom came in with his Thai generals and immediately walked to the far corner of the room, bending down and picking something up. "What the hell is this, Wonder Woman?" He held up a single rose petal in his fingers, looking at me ferociously.* Kam pood mai oke, dto nan chan mai me reng[119]. *P Tom walked over to me slowly. He bent down until his face was next to mine, then broke into a twisted smile. "I need you to tell me where…" He broke off as three rose petals spiraled out of the air, landing at his feet. One of the Thai generals started speaking to P Tom rapidly in English. I don't know what the man said. When P Tom looked back at me, his eyes were wide. "You did this?" My eyes locked for a moment with that of the English-speaking general. He gave me the slightest of nods, and I said, "Yes." They had told P Tom that my powers as a* ma du *were increasing rapidly, that I could now make objects appear at will. Was that Thai general a White Elephant, too? There are many things I'll never understand. At 10:59 p.m. that night, I was with S. again, and my rose lady was approached by a drifting* samlor *on Ratchawithi road. Its passenger was a groomed Thai man with a bottle of beer in his hand. He directed the driver to stop and started fishing in his pocket. By the time he came up with some coins, examined the rose lady's selection, and finally took the stem of a long rose between his fingers, a whole minute had passed. The* samlor *continued east to* Tapae Gate, *floated into moat traffic, then U-turned onto the outer road. They went past Suriwong Theater, and I winced with the memories. The* samlor *dropped the man off in front of a jewelry shop, which he*

---

[119] *Kam pood mai oke, dto nan chan mai me reng:* "I didn't have the energy to speak." (คำพูดไม่ออกตอนนั้นฉันไม่มีแรง)

apparently owned. He looked a little drunk as he stumbled inside. S. called me back to the room, beaming. I had found my first White Elephant, she said. She appeared to understand many things about this stranger. It was hard to keep up with everything S. told me. Two hundred years ago, he was a civil servant under the jao fa[120] *of Chiang Mai and owned lots of land. In that time, S. told me, it was common for landowners to take serfs as collateral for debts owed to them. In the case of this man, however, he made merit by presenting each of his serfs to the wat near his home. All of those serfs became high-ranking monks, and they were sought out by both Burmese and Lanna governors and princes for advice. The man had a good reputation for kind deeds. S. was flipping through a thick, dusty book as she spoke. I asked her where it was from. She winked at me and said she was also known as a librarian. I nodded my head and looked at the floor, not understanding. I wanted to know what would happen next. In his case, S. told me, the man in the jewelry shop would be guided to protect the energy of three of Chiang Mai's most important temples. He would keep their doorways pure. I tried asking more questions, but S. only chuckled, closing the book. A cloud of dust curled to the ceiling. "You are as curious as Wan Wan," she remarked. Wan Wan? That was the Burmese girl I had seen in the hallway, the one whose eyes never left me, the one whose heart and mind were my own. That was Khun Sa's granddaughter. She was being held by the Thai-American alliance as part of an agreement that Khun Sa had made with the military. "Wan Wan is a powerful soul," S. said in a lowered voice, leaning toward me with sharp eyes. "She was a Burmese princess who lost her life during the raids of Chiang Mai's seven princes. Her karma in this life is to receive their penitence, so one of them gifts her lottery numbers." That was the spirit of Jao Khanan Kawila, she added, the eldest prince and former* phraya[121] *of Lampang. All of the money that Wan Wan won in the lottery was being used by the Archons against the*

---

[120] *Jao fa:* Local prince (เจ้าฟ้า)

[121] *Phraya:* Ruler (พระยา)

White Elephants. Of course, the military officers at the base took profits, too. Khun Sa knew nothing of the situation, and they wished for it to stay that way. They will take my life so quickly if they ever read this. You have no idea, and you probably never will. There is a cost to everything. In the next few weeks, S. became furtive. We stopped viewing the rose ladies and White Elephants in Chiang Mai. Instead, I was spying on the military officers of Nakhon Phanom, sometimes even P Tom. And when I was with them, they used my viewing skills like a surveillance system, scanning the entire base for any disturbance. There were several times I saw S. in the corridors, but I never said anything. Didn't they know who she was? What did they know? What did anyone know? I could feel that Wan Wan was watching me, waiting for me. She was screaming through the walls. I could hear it in my mind like a siren. They were hurting her, but in my innocence, I couldn't understand why. I only knew she needed my help. Everyone was fighting over her like a valuable phra kru-ang[122]. *What they didn't know was that her traumas were my own. Every time they put something inside of her, I felt it. Every time an officer stood in front of her, unfastening his belt, my heart started thumping. When the bullet passed through the last officer's skull and his body slumped onto the bed, my body jumped out of the way, and her scream was my own. We were the same girl. We were lying there in the dark with something hot and wet pouring onto our left leg like a fountain. Noise filled the hallways, gunshots and groans. Someone grabbed us and ran into the light of the hallway. Our breath was one for only a moment more. There was a fleeting light that blinded us and made us feel bigger than the world. The light was our home. When I realized I wasn't with her anymore, I was being carried in the opposite direction on an officer's shoulder. I turned my head to get a look with all the strength I had. What I saw made me scream, and I kept screaming. I am screaming even now. You will never hear it, but I will never stop. You know my name. Everyone does.*

---

[122] *Phra kruang:* Amulet (พระเครื่อง)

But that name is like a band-aid trying to cover a wound that only gets bigger, and bigger, and bigger...

CHAPTER NINE

It was the morning after a storm. Chiang Mai shone like a polished gem as we made our way to the immigration offices, the fallen leaves smeared on the sidewalks being the only evidence of last night's fury. High gusts of wind had slammed my shutters with a thud at midnight—I was prepared for a visitor, someone bearing numbers from an "Oleon station." Nothing of the sort, of course. Just Quik's *wah* guitar cutting through my speaker with serene novas of sound. I exhaled tobacco smoke, nodding my head. As he enumerated his reasons for not wanting to party with scufflers, I tried to imagine my reaction if Master Elezon or the librarian showed up at my door, blown in from the mountain winds.

Beneath the city's placid guise, there was a growing feeling of unrest (according to social media, anyway). The national networks had been rocked with new revelations about Malila's *karsai* massage parlors. The families of several young girls had come forward with allegations that some of Malila's investors, all military officers, were known sex offenders. There were pictures, lurid accounts, multiple witnesses. Thai media had prioritized the scandal and taken it upon itself to stir public outrage. In turn, the student protests were given new life, having found fresh scapegoats. The news programs only served to amplify the details of the scandal, which all seemed to originate from a small circle of social media channels whose follower numbers were boosted overnight. "The Chinese manipulate Thai people again," was Nim's ineffable analysis. I had a joke about the military *needing a hand* that I wisely kept to myself.

The two of us had arrived at immigration a little before 9 a.m. Queues of mumbling foreigners had already formed, most of them clutching heavy stacks of paperwork that would, most likely, win them only three more months in the Thai Kingdom at best. When you go to the walking street market on a mild Sunday in November, it's amusing to look at these foreigners and imagine the sky-high tower of documents that has granted them a fleeting enjoyment of fried crickets. For local Thais, observing the immigration scene is probably like seeing a zoo of *farangs*, all shapes and sizes, some of undetermined phyla. They run in and out, many of them wild-eyed, forever needing one more document, one more useless badge of authentication, which is nonetheless paramount. Teachers, diplomats, vagabonds, veterans, retirees—all wincing under the lens of examination, knowing their lives in Chiang Mai could be shattered like a well-placed vase, even on a beautiful morning like this one.

Personally, I was feeling like a VIP. I was at immigration with no passport, with no need to stand in a queue. *Pure bliss.* It felt like skipping security at an airport and proceeding straight to the gate without having to fumble around with my belt. In keeping with the analogy, though, the catch was that we had no clue as to our flight destination: *Dubai? Costa Rica? Mars?* The monks hadn't confirmed Nim's status as Suphankanlaya, technically. What the hell kind of a government officer was there who could? (Amid the banalities of immigration, no less.)

Nim wasn't necessarily the warmest of companions on this

morning, either. Her mood was formal, curt, joyless. I thought it might have something to do with Malila, though I didn't dare ask. She wore a forest-green sport coat with prominent lapels and a low-cut black blouse to match a white-polka-dotted black skirt. Her hair was pulled back tight with some loose strands of hair falling across her temples, and the hoop earrings in her ears made her seem unapproachable. My presumptive princess was captive to her phone notifications, as was everyone else. Between the officers stamping paperwork and the distracted *farangs*, everyone seemed to have equal disregard for one another.

An automated voice sounded out queue numbers in English and Thai at random intervals. Twisting around in my hard-backed chair, I scanned the room, looking for relief from the boredom. Just then, a guy walked in with a screen-printed graphic of DJ Quik on his black tee. *Of course.* He didn't strike me as the sociable type, however.

My thoughts wandered to Open Source and our new Chiang Mai track. *When will that be done?*

"Prism!"

I jerked around. It was Eric B, standing with his hand outstretched. Next to him was an anonymous hottie smiling wanly. (Not the one from Topic 36, I noticed.) Eric B was dressed to the nines; his companion was barely dressed at all.

"Even rappers need visa extensions," he grinned, performing a *wai* to Nim in exquisite manner.

"Not this time, actually," I blurted.

"Wait, so what are you guys here for, then?"

"Well, uh—" I fumbled for an explanation. "Nim is meeting with a government officer and I just came along for support."

"Oh, okay," said Eric B, a note of uncertainty in his voice. "Good boyfriend."

"What about you guys?" As I asked the question, a number droned from the loudspeakers, and Eric B's companion immediately patted him on the arm before walking to the counter. The click of her high heels drew a rare glance from Nim.

"So is this your...*visa* lady, or...?"

"Sorta," laughed Eric B. "Honestly, I changed my Tinder bio a few nights ago. Check it out: *would you like to audition as my immigration secretary?* Had all these chicks in my inbox immediately."

"You *would* do something like that. What's her deal?"

"I don't know," the playboy said, scratching his head. "She said she's from Lamphun, but she has a cousin here at immigration or something. Accelerating the process a little." He winked.

"Let me guess," I replied. "Her hair is long but not long enough, and she says her skin is too dark, even though she's whiter than I am."

"Prism, you've been here too long," chuckled Eric B. "But yeah! I asked her: 'You think you're darker than me?' She said, 'If I go in the sun, I'm the same color.'" He punctuated the statement with raised eyebrows.

Some commotion behind the immigration desks drew our attention. Two officers were standing in front of a disheveled American. His face beet red, he was holding his open passport in the air and striking it repeatedly with a finger, desperately arguing their decision in pidgin English. Eric B and I exchanged a wide-eyed look: it was none other than the grouch from Topic 36. *This guy.* He looked to be on the losing end of another Thai incident.

"Visa finished on thirteenth; thirteenth was Saturday; I come on Saturday but immigration closed. Cannot renew. So now I come again..."

"No, no, no—*finished!*" declared the annoyed officer. "You are leave Thailand, visa expire!"

"Damn," Eric B said next to me. "This fool's karma is sub-zero..."

The unwritten code of *kraeng jai*[123] stipulates, among other things, that a foreigner can never openly confront a Thai person, let alone an official. The grouch's ignorance was his misfortune. In a childish spasm of rage, he turned and kicked a plastic trash can near the officers before attempting to storm out. A wave of shock and indignation passed through the rest of the immigration employees, each of them at their desks with mountains of paper in front of them. There was an audible gasp; some of the women shot up from their chairs as if standing at attention, their jaws taut and dark eyes glaring daggers. The grouch had made a grave error. Three security guards converged on him, corralling his arms. Rows of heads turned as the grouch was escorted to the door and effectively deported. "It's a kangaroo court!" were his parting yells.

"So stupid," Nim commented, as if her beauty sleep had been interrupted.

"See," Eric B cracked, "that's why I got an immigration secretary. Fuck all that!"

One of the officers walked over to us with a bright smile, as if nothing had happened. It was time for our appointment. Eric B and I bumped fists in a quick farewell. I could feel the questions he left unspoken, and I wondered how much he had heard from Concise and Source about what happened at the show. I didn't have time to give it much thought.

Nim and I followed the officer through a door at the back of the office, then up a phosphorescent stairwell. We found ourselves in a long, sterile hallway ornamented with pictures of the current king. I checked—none of the calendars said 1983. We reached a

---

[123] *kraeng jai:* Thai social code of manners and etiquette (เกรงใจ)

door, and the officer turned to us, speaking to Nim in Thai. He had to pat us down before he could let us in. Having done so, the officer opened the door and extended one arm in courtesy. "*Chern luy*[124], *krub!*"

Our first thought was that the room was just like any other office in such a building except that nobody was sitting at the desk and two warm lamps were the only source of light. A large Ganesh sculpture stood against the wall. Sitting on the desk were a takeout bag of *pad krapow*[125] and a carton of chocolate milk.

I heard Nim's breath catch in her throat, and I turned to look. Even in military uniform, without the cat ears, I recognized who it was instantly. *Malila.* Without a word, the makeup phenom walked briskly to her desk and sat down. I looked at Nim in shock, not understanding. Her mouth hung half-open helplessly. Probably only five minutes before, Malila had been a pretty face on Nim's screen—now that face was on a government official, staring back at her from behind a desk.

"*Sawadee jao*[126], please have a seat," Malila chirped, breaking the spell. "I am Jeerawan Ratcharot, and today I am to consult for your lottery case, *na kha.* You know me as another person, I know. But today you must treat to me like you've never seen me before, and never will see me again. Okay?"

I could feel Nim's quantum brain recalibrating next to me. She was starting to recover from the shock of meeting her idol under such bizarre circumstances. It was a new code for her to crack, a game within the lottery game she was keen to master. Nim was a natural winner, of course, and her confidence and poise were never

---

[124] *Chern luy:* "Please come in!" (เชิญ)

[125] *Pad krapow:* A rice dish with meat stir-fried in basil. (ผัดกะเพรา)

[126] *Jao:* An expression of politeness native to northern Thailand (เจ้า)

long absent. She unleashed a torrent of Thai by means of introducing herself. There are some games, however, not made for the average winner to play. Malila cut her off abruptly.

"Sorry, *kha*, I must ask for speaking English today, for him." Malila made the demand without even a glance in my direction. She paused for a moment, a troublesome thought disturbing the surface of her elegant face. "You—you aren't like *her*, you aren't close! Where is your..."

"Sorry?" said Nim after an awkward pause.

"Forget it," replied Malila quickly, forcing a smile that she quickly withdrew. Her hands were folded rigidly in front of her on the desk. She was an actor of some kind, I realized. Normally we saw her "second face," some kind of too-cute-for-school persona. Malila's attractiveness now had a more controlling aspect to it, yet she was also fragile—so fragile that the slightest noise might shatter her composure into pieces. Nonetheless, she seemed to stare *into* us in a way that deeply creeped me out. Was this how luck felt?

"First, *Khun*[127] Nim," Malila continued, "has the lottery game satisfied you so far?"

"Yes, everything fine," replied Nim, now turning a pair of lottery tickets in her hand. "But I want to know—"

"Who the man in your dream is, of course," Malila interjected, sounding like a Thai version of Siri. "That is Phra Naresuan, and I think your boyfriend know this already."

Nim glanced at me with a raised eyebrow, crossed her legs, then looked back to Malila. "Means I am Suphankanlaya?"

"There are many possibilities," replied Malila, "and that is one of them. To be honest, it is not *most* important to know, now. You have a responsibility you cannot understand, *na kha*. The lottery

---

[127] *Khun*: Equivalent to Mr./Ms. (คุณ)

selected you because you can to help Phra Naresuan most quickly. Now he is trapped by the contract he make in the past. When he is set free—"

A noise in the hallway immediately silenced the strange woman, and her eyes darted in space, listening.

"When he is set free," she resumed, "good people will have power again. Timelines are improved. It is too much for me to explain, *Khun* Nim. But I think you know how your life has changed, right? Three years ago, you remember?"

"Whaaat!" exclaimed Nim. "How you know that?"

"When the monk asked you to change your name, you changed your life path."

"Wait," I interjected, "Nim *isn't* your real name?"

"It's her second name, *kha*," Malila answered, looking at me for the first time. "But also real. The monk told her that *Nim* would give her a life of fortune. Yes, and now look at where you are. This name create the energy of service, that is why Phra Naresuan comes to you now. Your luck—"

"—is an instrument of reinventing the past?"

"Excuse me?" Malila's eyes flashed in recognition, fixing on me.

"I said—"

"Okay, it's okay. I understand now," she said cryptically. "But *Khun* Prism, your only concern should be listening to your mother." The statement was a confirmation, but Malila's delivery made it feel like a dagger. Nim instinctively patted my knee in consolation. Malila was eyeing me queerly. "You think your girlfriend is the only one who has the instrument you mentioned?"

"What do you know about my mother?"

"She is learning that she can change the world through you. That is all I can tell you now," said Malila. I felt a chill shoot up my spine. Malila took out a hand mirror and started applying foundation. Was she really psychic, or was it just cosmetics?

"Ah, P Jeerawan," Nim exclaimed, "the matte color is my favorite, too."

A condescending kind of humor passed over Malila's face, but she ignored the remark. "*Khun* Nim, do you still have the lottery money?"

"Yes, *kha*."

"You must divide the money between nine different temples in provinces of Phayao and Lampang. Give all as merit. You must go alone, and it must be completed within two weeks. Then the gates of Wat Luang Ratcha will be reopened, and Phra Naresuan's mission will be complete."

"Wat Luang Ratcha is where?" Nim had started to respond in Thai, but caught herself.

"Now it is nowhere, but you must find it. It is where it always has been, *na kha*. Once you have given merit to all nine temples, Phra Naresuan will walk through its gates again. The *silajaruk*[128] stone will stand in the unseen doorway."

Nim and I exchanged a puzzled look. It sounded like some *hot* mumbo-jumbo, but Malila spoke with the precision of someone pulling records from a computer database. Her speech was rapid and accompanied by a disconcertingly blank expression.

"The key to the temple," added Malila, "is the key *that it's in*. Okay? I cannot tell you anything more. Give me your tickets," she instructed, reaching a hand out to Nim.

The latter did so with a furrowed brow. Malila drew her chair to the Ganesha sculpture behind her, put her hands on either side of the elephant head, and detached it from the body. Reaching into

---

[128] *Silajaruk*: Ceremonial stone historically used to mark official property (ศิลาจารึก)

the safe, she pulled out several bound stacks of 1,000-*baht* bills then slid them across the desk. The multi-trunked head was then restored to its body.

"Congratulations, *Khun* Nim, you've won another one hundred thousand *baht* in Thai lottery," Malila announced dryly.

"I don't understand," replied Nim, shaking her head with some annoyance.

"Your lucky numbers," Malila said, "were 231, 201, 221, 114, 718. You will receive two more lucky numbers: 120 and 381."

"And why do you know?"

"*Khun* Nim, you cannot to spell *Wat Luang Ratcha* without A-T-C-H-A. They aren't lottery numbers. They're letters of the name of your mission. Can you see? We can't wait for another month, so we expedite your winnings, *na kha*."

"Hmm," said a now openly skeptical Nim, tapping her nails on the desk. "I don't play games with fraud, na. Where this money come from, P Malila?"

"You want to keep the money you win, I understand *na kha*. We decide you may keep five percent of your earnings. Take it if you want. You chose this mission, *Khun* Nim. The business of your karma is not for us to concern. And you may call me *Malila* if you want, but *Malila* is not real, and only the fool believe everything they hear—"

Nim promptly shoveled the cash into her Gucci bag. Her pride was wounded. A voice had entered my head as Malila spoke, however. It said: *She will need you to complete the circle of merit.*

That was all—it was almost like a radio transmission in thought form. Malila suddenly grabbed the far edge of the desk, tightening her hold until her knuckles were white. Her eyes were closed. She was now speaking in an unfamiliar tongue, a series of high-pitched sounds rolling from her throat like complex beeping, mixed with prolonged vowel sounds.

We quickly rose in alarm and started backing our way toward the door. Malila's eyes flew open, and her posture relaxed. Her chest was heaving. "You don't know the games they play," she suddenly snapped. Malila rose from her chair and looked around the room, then walked unsteadily toward a framed painting of a military official on the wall, her back to us. Nim and I stood rooted to the spot. We watched as she traced her finger along the edge of the frame like she was touching a rare thing of value. Silence filled the room. When Malila turned to us again, a weird smile was playing on her lips, a smile of sadness.

"Don't you wish you have power to float across the valleys, mountains—just once, or a few times? I mean—feeling the air under your feet, rise into the cloud, disappear...?"

Nodding like bobblehead dolls, we quickly turned to leave, with Nim somehow managing a *wai*. A brisk "sawadee kha" followed us as we fled the room, and that was how we left Malila, the loneliest, oddest, and most complicated woman with a million followers you could imagine.

My offended girlfriend's summation was less sympathetic. "*E dok*[129]," she muttered to herself bitterly as we made our way out of the immigration building.

I didn't say anything. The mundane scene of visa-stamping again surrounded us. Deliberations, assessments, negotiations, verdicts. Faces drained of spirit, heels twitching on the floor. We shouldered our way past a gentleman in the doorway whose additional application forms were always the final step everyone forgot.

Finally, the open air, the sky's ruffled clouds. In the parking lot was a rose merchant holding bouquets of many colors. I shot a

---

[129] *E dok:* "Bitch." (อีดอก)

look at Nim, who seemed ready to cry. I paid five *baht* for a single rose, lifting it to her nose with care.

CHAPTER TEN

In the dream, I was moving on tiptoes into a dark room when I heard the sound of glass shattering. Small figures with bright skin were fleeing the room in a mysterious panic. One had dropped something and stopped short, turning around. An unknown fragrance filled my nose as I stepped over shards of glass, trying to get a look at the figure. Oval eyes dominated its face, and the chin came to a point. I made a motion to pick up what was on the floor. That was when the figure lost its physical nature, turned into a cloud, and was sucked into the opposite doorway. Lights came on; I was alone. Broken glass twinkled like chunks of quartz. I saw a book on the floor and picked it up, turning to a random page. The first: "IT'S." The second: "FUNNY." The third: "HOW." Turning from page to page, the rest of the message read: "...*one pencil can scramble timelines.*" I knew this from somewhere—a TV show?—but couldn't place it.

Waking up resolved my ignorance but failed to relieve the confusion. Nim was lying next to me, half-asleep. My hand instinctively stroked her bare leg and she stirred into my arms. Our gyrating bodies filled the spaces our dreams left empty, as if to consummate what our minds couldn't understand. We plunged toward a conclusion we tried to stave off—and then, with a sigh, it was reached.

Daylight peeked through the curtains to banish our dreams. We were lying naked on the bed, looking at the ceiling, at ease. She, too, had dreamed, but the lottery man's appearance had disappointed her. Everything he told her, including the number, had confirmed what Malila told us. Or so it seemed. *Ja tom arrai bong ti rak?*[130] For days, Nim had been deliberating on whether or not to follow the makeup artist's instructions. In her mind, the idea that Malila, the monks, and the military were all in on some elaborate scam involving ghosts wasn't the worst part. No—worse was the fact that Malila had brushed off the idea of Nim's royal origins with scorn. Maybe she wasn't Suphankanlaya, after all.

Nim needed *that* to be true. The money didn't matter so much to her as it did that she was *entitled* to the money, owing to her higher status. If she was Suphankanlaya, that meant there was a reason for the estrangement from her mother, which released her from a certain personal responsibility for their relationship issues. Over the years, her mother had tried to come back into her life several times, and had even asked for loans as her daughter became more successful. Nim could retrofit this story of being a reincarnated queen in a way that explained her childhood troubles; it validated her feeling that her mother was of a lower station, a peasant incapable of caring for a princess—not simply a woman with too many issues to love her only daughter.

"You never told me you had another name," I ventured, tracing circles around her belly button.

"*Ben shuh khou, tom mai Nim kuan bok Prism[131]?*"

---

[130] *Ja tom arrai bong ti rak?:* "What are you gonna do, babe?" (จะทำอะไรบ้างทีรัก)
[131] *Ben shuh khou, tom mai Nim kuan bok Prism:* "It's my old name, why should I have told you?" (เป็นชื่อเก่าทำไมนิมควรบอก...)

"I dunno, because it's not your real name?"

"*Ow*[132], it is my real name, na," she insisted, pushing my hand away. "We filed papers in Chonburi *laew*[133]."

"Isn't it weird to have a different name?"

"I get used to it. You know, the monks gave me many choices for the name." Nim sat up to pull her hair into a bun. "The thing Malila say is true about that, but I still think she *gahok*[134]."

"What did the monks tell you?"

"*Bok wa...ta brien chua, ja me sombot neh non, ja hai chok dee kong chan nai chiwit neh non.*[135]"

"Hmm. I think they were right. *Chai mai?*" I gave her a reassuring peck on the cheek.

"But what if Malila is lying to me? If I am the queen, why I should give all my money? You know, luck is not given to poor people. Everything have the reason, you know? In Thai, only royalty can be royalty. That's why I not angry my mom, only pity her."

"I think, if you give the money to those temples, your luck will be even better than before."

Nim only shook her head, unconvinced. I decided not to tell her about the mental message from Malila. Several more days would pass before the storm broke and the decision to go to Lampang was made for her. Maybe it was better that way.

Hop reappeared around this time, right after we had gone to immigration, and right before everything that was to happen next.

---

[132] *Ow:* Expression of worry or concern (อ้าว)

[133] *Laew:* Already (แล้ว)

[134] *Gahok:* Liar (โกหก)

[135] *Bok wa...ta brien chua, ja me sombot neh non, ja hai chok dee kong chan nai chiwit neh non:* "They said if I change my name I will be guaranteed fortune, it will guarantee luck in my life."

(บอกว่าถ้าเปลี่ยนชื่อจะมีสมบัติแน่นอนก็เลยจะให้โชคดีของฉันในชีวิตแน่นอน)

He had been in Bangkok since the night he'd barreled into Topic 36 and, from what I could gather, it was Hop's obsession with winning the lottery that had led him to the Siamese city of angels. His entire trip can be captured succinctly in four images. One: Hop behind the wheel of his green beat-up Volkswagen, a spliff simmering between his lips, with tiered pagodas silhouetted against a horizon of amber on either side. Two: Hop standing under a towering overpass, forlornly watching ambulance doors slam shut as robed monks gather at the site of tainted cement. Three: Hop kneeling at the foot of an altar with flowers around his neck as pedestrians pour into a nearby MK Restaurant, the "M" flashing on the neon sign. Four: Hop gently accepting a vinyl record from the hands of a woman whose face is hidden, her skin appearing to coruscate with color. Each image is a bead attached to the same thread, somehow, so bear with me as I attempt to explain.

It was no secret that Nim's accomplishments in the lottery had aroused Hop's ambitions. Not long after the night of Topic 36, Hop had jumped into his van and driven all the way to Bangkok, an assortment of amulets swinging from his rearview mirror. First, though, he had to return the black dog.

Hop had been driving around with the poor animal for two weeks, thinking its presence might be the missing key. He had discovered the black dog outside of a convenience store. In exchange for copious amounts of *gai tod*[136], the dog was willing to play the role of good-luck charm indefinitely.

When Hop finally returned to the convenience store, however, he realized the dog belonged to the store owner. After cooling the man's temper with donations and a trio of red Fantas outside of the shop's spirit house, Hop sat down to talk with him. It turned

---

[136] *Gai tod:* Fried chicken (ไก่ทอด)

out that his son was married to a woman in Bangkok who sup-
ported a certain Buddhist organization involved with helping the
victims of car accidents. Why shouldn't Hop, the man suggested,
go down to Bangkok and volunteer for the organization? Everyone
knew that the license plates in automobile accidents could be used
as lucky numbers in the lottery.

And so it was. After a thirteen-hour drive, Hop found himself
in the stifling clamps of *Krungthep*[137], despite the fact that there were
times along the way he'd forgotten where he was going, and indeed, the appearance of skyscrapers and traffic gave him a jolt.
They say that the city, sinking back into the earth as it is, has already
met its end, that there is no difference between its living and dead,
that the spirit of the Chao Praya river has already been laid to rest
in the urban tomb of asphalt. (The capital's dead, it would seem,
are much busier than the Chiang Mai living.) Hop had made no
prior arrangements, no plans. His luck was such, however, that it
didn't matter, and he spent that night on the top floor of a
shophouse near Chinatown. Hop is always lucky enough to get by,
but not lucky enough to *not need* luck to get by.

Now we've come to the second image bead. To understand the
purpose of the Buddhist organization for which Hop decided to
volunteer, you must first consider that Bangkok is said to be swirling with furious *phii*[138], and that there isn't one misfortune that
can't be ascribed to their vengeful campaigns. Bangkok is a city
that can't escape its dead. So it follows that, when there is a horrific
accident, monks must rush to the scene in order to perform the
proper rites, to make sure that another upset ghost doesn't threaten
to turn the city upside down. They sift through twisted metal

---

[137] *Krungthep:* Bangkok (กรุงเทพ)
[138] *Phii:* Ghosts (ผี)

before the paramedics arrive, reattaching limbs, murmuring mantras. This is the situation in which Hop, still getting his bearings, somehow found himself.

At first, he jotted down every license plate number he saw. Soon, he was overtaken by disgust—not only at the alarming carnage of crash scenes, but also the boredom that came from sitting in the black van with other Buddhist body snatchers, waiting, and waiting, *and waiting* for the collision that would send another soul on an angry rampage.

Hop found one of the license plate numbers tattooed on the naked thigh of a Vietnamese girl at a massage parlor, which was enough to shift his attention from the nightmare of car wrecks to the low-lit sensuality of Chinatown brothels—he reasoned that the girls' tattoos, if taken together, would contain the code of his fortune. This arduous inquiry on his part lasted for weeks. (With noodles hanging from his mouth, Hop handed me a crumpled piece of paper, marked up with numbers, drawings, names: the product of his research.) One morning, he realized that one of his amulets was gone. He'd been wearing it at the massage parlor the night before but couldn't remember if he had ever taken it off. Hop stumbled back to the site, but it was too early in the morning. Its iron grill was locked shut. Eyes squinting in the cruel morning sun, my friend started walking nowhere in particular.

The markets blurred into a mirage around Hop. He was thirsty. A *cha giew*[139] stall appeared on the curb, and he jingled through his pockets for fifteen *baht*. Someone bumped into him—Hop turned to apologize, but no one was there. He slurped the cool, sugary tea 'til his brain tingled.

The tea lady was extending a wreath of jasmine flowers,

---

[139] *Cha giew:* Green tea (ชาเขียว)

pointing at a spot farther down the street. Hop looked. A tall statue of white marble stood like a tree among the swirling stalls, a mound of flowers piled at its base. Maybe the lost amulet, Hop reasoned, would turn up after he made merit to the Chinese goddess. It wasn't just any amulet, after all: it was from the famed Wat Kam Cha Nod in Udon Thani, where people received winning lottery numbers from the lake-dwelling *payanok*[140]. That brings us to the third image bead.

Hop threw the wreath around his neck and marched toward the marble statue. It was positioned on a street corner beneath the red signs that bristled with yellow Mandarin. Kneeling down at the statue's base, he was surprised no one else was kneeling there. Instead, people stumbled into him, yelping in alarm. They were pouring into an MK Restaurant on the opposite corner; some turned back to give Hop a questioning glare. Soon the glares turned into laughs. A small circle of mockery formed around Hop, and began to grow in size. He turned back to the marble statue in confusion, but there was only a pile of garbage teeming with flies.

Eyung wa[141]?! At that moment, an electrical zap filled the air. The "M" on the restaurant's sign flickered off, on, and off again. There were cries of disbelief. In the ensuing confusion, Hop heard a hissing sound and looked up. A strange woman was beckoning to him from the adjoining shopfront, two cats curling around her legs.

Hop, brushing the hair from his face, found himself in a record shop. Along with thousands of records, there were various instruments hung on the walls, massive crystal geodes of quartz, shungite, citrine, and malachite, and clocks of different shapes and sizes whose hands raced madly in a blur. The woman, Hop said,

---

[140] *Payanok:* Serpent people (พญานาค)

[141] *Eyung wa:* "What the hell?" (อิหยังวะ)

was neither young nor old, but she wore a loose tunic gracing her slender body, and she held some kind of tall stringed instrument with a gourd at the bottom, perhaps a ngoni. Hop felt an unaccountably familiar sense of peace.

The woman, leading him through a doorway of hanging beads, sat him down on a long sofa next to a glass table. Her name was Lanna. "You have already experienced what you are seeking," she whispered. "That is why your true fortune is concealed."

She didn't say anything more for the space of an hour, only holding Hop's attention with the mellifluous sounds of the ngoni in her lap. The cats stalked in, taking up their positions on either side of Hop. One was white, the other black. Their names were something like Elezana and Oomanil—Hop got the impression that they, too, were listening, conveying. The instrument sounded much louder than it should have. Was there an amplifier hidden somewhere? There were no wires or speakers in sight.

Lanna broke the silence by admitting there were many others like her on earth, that they were working together in secret to open doorways between their realms and ours. She said many other oblique things, most of which Hop couldn't remember.

Finally, she ceased playing, placing the ngoni to the side. The cats fled to either corner of the room, twisting their necks around to clean their backsides. Lanna gazed directly into Hop's eyes with intense power, moving herself closer on the sofa. Her hands stroked his hair softly. She took Hop's hand and fixed it to the roundness of her left breast, sighing.

Hop, shocked and aroused, felt her hand slipping into his pants, clutching his erection and massaging it with the same skill that she had plucked the ngoni strings. Never breaking eye contact, her lips grew redder than the shell of a mangosteen, and with one swing of a leg, she had mounted Hop and guided his penis to the threshold of her moist opening. Lanna slid herself down its full length and began jerking in circular motions, moaning. As the rosebuds of her nipples rose and fell in front of him, Hop became aware of two things: one, there was a man in the doorway watching, a smile on his face, and two, the color of Lanna's skin had changed from white to a pigmented pink. That was his last memory before a period of lost time.

When he finally came to, Hop was dressed in different clothes and a cat's paw was playfully batting at his chin. He sat up, taking note of the brown tunic that had replaced his t-shirt and jeans. The tender, ancient sound of the ngoni strings again filled the room, but this time there was no one playing. Stacks of reggae records were scattered across the floor, and orbs of blue light darted around the ceiling. Lanna and the strange man were arranging the records into boxes, seemingly in a hurry. Her skin was somehow now a kind of rosy tan color, but Hop said he was sure it was the same woman. He realized she was what the Thais call *nang sam phiu*[142], although their existence had been deemed a myth. The orbs of blue light seemed to have something to do with the music. Invisible ngoni strings pervaded the air around them.

We have reached the fourth image bead of Hop's stay in Bangkok. Lanna stood up and turned to my friend. She was now wearing a hooded white robe of silk that contrasted with her new skin. Hop prepared for another seduction, but Lanna showed no such urge. She only handed him a record whose cover was faded and peeling at the edges. *No, Dread Can't Dead/Jam Stitchon.* Hop took it into his hands gently, regarding it with hesitant admiration. Lanna placed one hand on his shoulder in the manner of a fond old friend.

---

[142] *Nang sam phiu:* "Three-skin lady." (นางสามผิว)

"We release you back into your realm, to which you will bear the keys to our doorways. The portals of your earth have been altered and reshaped long before we became involved. The silajaruk *stones must be restored to their original positions for the portals of light to be reopened. Sound can be used in the manner of a paintbrush, or in that of a sword. When you learn the skill of each, you will have completed that which you've set out to do."*

Having expressed all of this, Lanna gave Hop a nod and stepped away. Brief business arrangements were made between Hop and the strange man in the tunic. Money was put in Hop's hand—more than he'd ever had—and it was announced that he should use it to open his own record store once he was home.

Seven or eight crates of reggae records were put into Hop's care. He felt something brush across his neck. Turning around, he saw that the two cats were sitting together on a shelf. The black one was motioning to him with an outstretched paw, its whiskered face parting in a soundless *meow*. And just like that, Hop was standing out on a Chinatown sidewalk again, crates of reggae music at his feet. According to his phone, Hop had been in that single shop for a day and a half.

It should be pointed out that this is all a translation of a translation, a flawed version of a story with missing chapters, gaps. Hop's English was always more capable than Nim's, of course, but still patchy at best. He was overdependent on certain words like "opportunity," the usage of which Hop redefined in his attempt to articulate urges and choices. For example, his time at the brothel was a "new opportunity for success," and these kinds of "opportunities" seemed to always multiply around him. In listening to Hop, too, I sometimes got lost in wondering if one detail was linked to another—for a time, I thought the two cats were responsible for the sound of music, which led me down a fruitless train of thought. His telling of the story kept getting interrupted as I urged him to revisit earlier details. For all these hiccups, though, it was clear that Hop had run into the same outfit of door-opening cosmonauts that I had.

We were sitting in the back of an empty Burmese diner on Suthep road having lunch—I can't forget it. My plate was filled with blue rice and tea leaf salad, my teeth busy crunching their way through sesame seeds stuck to juicy bits of tomato. Hop was working on some kind of fish soup with loads of chili. His manner struck me as sheepish and subdued, and I noticed that his shrill cackle was edged with nervousness. Hop's silky hair was longer than before, and a curly goatee had sprouted from his chin. He pushed some coin-shaped objects to the center of the table.

"Magnets," he explained. "They were inside the boxes."

"With the reggae records?"

"Yep," Hop affirmed, curling a strand of hair around his ear. "Maybe shungite."

"What is that?" I asked, picking one up and turning it in my hand.

"I'm not sure. My uncle said it can protect from radiation."

"Hmm. So are you going to start a record shop now?"

"Maybe," Hop said, nodding. "I think I will call it *Lao Tay Arrom*[143]. For any mood, we can find the music."

"Awesome," I said, laughing and nodding. I took another bite of the tea leaf salad laden with peppers. "So you really had sex with that—alien?"

This time there was no laughter in response. "I think this experience had the effect on me. Strange effect, you know. Everything with electronics is changed. Very, very—*peculiar*. Lights turn off near me. You see? Look at your phone."

---

[143] *Lao Tay Arrom*: "Whatever The Feeling Is" (แล้วแต่อารมณ์)

Indeed, my device was flashing off and on in a way I'd never seen. I looked up at Hop, who was smiling strangely. He pointed at one of the magnets, and I attached it to the phone. It immediately stabilized, arriving at the home screen as usual. "What the—?" My questions, however, were meant for another time.

"*Ba-toh*[144]," Hop exclaimed, reading something on his screen. He held it up to me, and I found myself looking at a headline that made me jump out of the chair. There it was, in plain black and white: **Malila linked to government lottery scam with Chiang Mai woman.** I paid for the food and started running to Nim's apartment, which wasn't too far away. I didn't stop until I reached her door.

---

[144] *Ba-toh:* Expression of surprise (ป๊โธ)

CHAPTER ELEVEN

She wasn't there, of course. When I tried calling her number, it went straight to voicemail. Nim had already left Chiang Mai—that much was clear. It was even possible that she had left town days before the article was published. Her family connections were A-1. I slumped onto a couch in her condo's lobby and opened the *Bangkok Courier* article on my phone. I took screenshots, too:

> Arrest warrants for Malila, embattled social media icon, and a local Chiang Mai woman identified as Patchaporn Seng have been issued in the wake of a developing embezzlement case, according to Bangkok's Crime Suppression Division (CSD).
>
> The warrants, already approved by the Criminal Court, describe a far-reaching conspiracy within the military and government possibly linked to a sex trafficking ring based in Phetchabun. While it remains unknown how the conspirators have corrupted the national lottery, there is evidence that Ms. Seng has illicitly benefited from her close friendship with Malila.

Both women remain at large and their whereabouts are unknown. Although the role of Ms. Seng is uncertain, a CSD investigator has reported that she received hundreds of thousands of baht in the lottery within a span of three months. Those funds were then likely embezzled to a shell company. Police have promised to complete the arrests by the end of the week.

The CSD started monitoring Malila's activities closely after the Karsai scandal leaked into the press last month. This led to a series of reports which at least one official has described as "unforgivable." They narrate the actions of a deviant woman who enjoys access to some of the most influential officials in the National Lottery Bureau and Ministry of Finance.

It's not the first time that government officials have been tagged in lottery scandals. In 2003, it was revealed that civil servant Prem Phacharakhun had rigged the lottery and tipped off political allies, from whom he collected a share of the winnings. The scope of Malila's crimes is more serious, however. The CSD has expressed concern that the scrutiny will be "more than the government can handle."

The allegations have also reignited student protests. Yesterday, close to 3,000 students gathered on the campus of Chulalongkorn University to listen to activists' tales of government corruption. Riffing on her popularity as a makeup artist, one sign read: "Ask Malila: Democracy is Only Skin-Deep."

Arrest warrants. Hop and I decided to lay low at a friend's house for a few nights as we planned our next move. The shock of seeing

Nim's Thai name in print like that of a criminal was only eclipsed by my realization that the public was being intentionally misled. There was no "shell company." Before our meeting with Malila, Nim had received all the numbers in her dreams from what we presumed to be a ghost of national importance. Strange, but not far-fetched. I was confident that the lottery man wasn't some dreamworld embezzler working for the Lottery Bureau. How could Nim's situation be so grossly misrepresented in the press? We were clearly caught up in something bigger.

Malila, I intuited, was not who they said she was. I flashed back to our meeting at the immigration office. " 'Malila' is not real. Only fools believe everything they hear," were her exact words. Obviously, the *person* we had met was real, so I could only deduce that she was referring to the *persona* of Malila, the makeup icon. During our rendezvous, she was outside of that persona, presenting herself instead as a government employee.

For days after I read the article, my eyes were spinning in concentric circles like a character from *Tom and Jerry*. What in the hell were the implications of *that*? Why would the government have one of its agents pose as a social media makeup artist? And what could Malila have possibly done to become the target of a smear campaign that spanned the national networks?

Nim and I, thanks to the monks at Wat Doi Kham, had caught a glimpse through the looking glass of a kind of *un-Malila*. Now we had to wonder what the cost of that glimpse was.

Several days passed. I'd still heard nothing from Nim. Hop and I lazed around my friend's house, rolling tobacco spliffs on the deck, discussing the best course of action. It was hard to plan anything without knowing Nim's status. If she was on the temple circuit in Lampang, I felt obligated to be with her somehow. In the words of Malila, we had *a responsibility that we couldn't understand*, and the time frame seemed urgent.

Hop, on the other hand, reasoned that it was better to remain where we were in Mae Rim until the storm blew over. My friend Garrett and his wife lived in a remote part of the mountains, and their home was only accessible by a winding dirt road beset with rocks and grazing goats. The land was formerly logging territory which the government had eventually allowed people to cultivate and build houses on, partly to avoid mudslides. You were lucky to have a signal out there half the time—we were *in the cut*. Garrett was nice enough as a host, too. He was a chipper Baha'i from the Toronto area who did children's classes on Zoom, often with a guitar strapped around his burly neck, a broad smile fixed on his face.

The story of Malila and Ms. Seng wasn't blowing over, though. Each headline was more sensational and provocative, the bold letters growing sharper and sharper to open old wounds of mistrust in the prime minister, the throne, the various ministries. As days dragged on without any arrests, protests reached a fever pitch. In an outlandish twist, hundreds of students showed up outside Wat Doi Kham with their inflatable yellow duckies, now smeared with lipstick and blush. It was being reported that Ms. Seng had frequented the lottery temple, which a military whistleblower had suddenly announced was "fundamental" to the lottery conspiracy.

Old couples dressed in white were jeered at by hoards of democratic protesters, daring to break the temple's porcelain silence. For the first time in Thai history, its most sacred institutions were on trial, and Hop's advice appeared far more sensible than mine— was it worth traveling ninety kilometers east to Lampang at the risk of being deported, thrown in Thai prison, or worse? I knew *they knew* who I was, too.

When I saw an odd number buzzing my phone, finally, I had

no doubt who it was. Nim's frazzled voice reached my ear through a wall of static, a mixture of relief and desperation in her tone. She was somewhere between Lampang and Phayao; her Naresuan donation tour was underway.

"You know they're after you, right?"

"I don't think so, Prism. You know my uncle works for the police. He called to the Bangkok police department, and you know what? Nobody knew about any arrest warrant."

"What?"

"Yesss," she chuckled nervously. "It looks like everything is the *fake news*."

"This country is so confusing," I replied with a sigh. I'd missed hearing Nim's colorful voice.

"*Nan dee*[145]. But I want to tell you something. You remember about the temple *ti khou bok rou tang pai tom hai silajaruk*[146]?"

"Uh, Wat Luang…"

"Wat Luang Ratcha, *chai*. Prism, you know, Wat Luang Ratcha is gone. *Hai laew*[147]. They take it down many years ago."

"Great."

"Uhhh! How can we go na?"

"No idea, *krub*."

"Prism," Nim whined softly, losing her professional tone, "when will you come out here?"

"Do you think I should?"

"You have to, na."

I paused. "What does your family think about all this?"

Nim gave a sarcastic laugh. "They think I should leave the

---

[145] *Nan dee*: A phrase of agreement (นั่นดี)

[146] *Ti khou bok rou tang pai tom hai silajaruk:* "…where they told us we had to go and summon a stone?" (ทีเขาบอกเราต้องไปทำศิลาจารึก)

[147] *Hai laew:* "It's gone." (หายแล้ว)

country. Take my savings and leave."

"And…?"

"Who knows. *Chang meng!* Oii Prism, *yak kin moo ka tat yuu*[148]…"

Food always took precedence over other pressing matters in the Thai Kingdom, which in this case gave me an odd sense of comfort. I could feel Nim's stress through her chatter. Nonetheless, things were never quite what I thought they were in this country. Was the pursuit of Malila and Nim just another red herring circulating in the media? While the press raged on about her conduct, Nim was gliding from one temple to the next like a Chinese tourist, only complaining of her craving for *moo ka tat*. The biggest thing I had to worry about was her driving skills, it seemed. There was something else, too. When Nim mentioned having to leave the country, I realized consciously for the first time how inevitable our breakup was, one way or another. I'd known this since the beginning: our time together was like the lantern festival, radiant and brief.

If there are past lives, it would neatly explain why some relationships seem to break off in the middle while others appear to complete something that our memories can't recall. Ours was like that. In our case, perhaps all the love we made was simply a physical ritual required by our karmic contract, something incapable of creating new life, insofar as our bond was like a passing gesture between strangers who once exchanged words on a distant afternoon. That isn't to say I didn't love Nim, as nothing is possible without love. I only wish to point out that the thorns of her love weren't so sharp as to leave a scar. Something about my mother passing on, too, made it more difficult for me to avoid the voice

---

[148] *yak kin moo ka tat yuu:* "I want to eat some barbecue pork."
(อยากกินหมูกระทะอยู่)

of my conscience, especially in matters of love. The experience of losing her to the other side made life's pretenses intolerable. My relationship with Nim, of course, wasn't a pretense—it was a potent, fleeting thing, a butterfly on a branch, whose disappearance I had to accept not pursuing.

It was the place where this butterfly had led me that mattered.

We were lucky that Garrett was such a gracious host, because Hop was proving to be the strangest of guests. Lights typically flashed off and on as he walked between rooms. Phones would go haywire in Hop's presence. The Wi-Fi signal routinely crashed at his slightest of motions—if Hop lifted his leg, it had the domino effect of sending Garrett's lively Zoom calls into a tailspin (midballad), unable to be recovered for a space of half an hour. Hop's electrical influence not only turned things off but also extended to turning them on. Because of his forgetful nature, he often failed to notice these things.

One time, Peach—Garrett's Thai wife—had left some chocolate walnut cookies in the oven to cool. Some friends were coming over in the evening for a sing-along with Garrett, and Peach had been busy in the kitchen most of the day in preparation. Hop happened to wander in during a time Peach had left the house. The oven lights blinked on, Hop left, and when Peach returned, she found all of her cookies scorched into mounds of coal.

Baha'is, generally, are among the nicest people in the world, and this couple was no exception. They had a sense of humor about Hop being a walking power outage. I did notice them muttering prayers under their breath from time to time, likely of the Lord-grant-me-the-strength variety.

Although our stay with them was short, we developed some house rules. Hop had to stay in another room if one of us was on a call. He also couldn't play his reggae records after dark—the reason being that whenever Hop played one of those records from Bangkok, his presence seemed to amplify the sounds well beyond the capacity of the speaker system. Garrett, a musician himself, was especially fascinated by this. He found that Hop could amplify the sound of his guitar, too—just by standing within five feet. His shungite magnets, we learned, protected our devices from Hop's interference, although the hair on our arms still stood on end around him. Hop was a human microphone. Garrett took to calling him over for "prayer time" in the evening, after a stiff shot of whiskey.

The news of Gabe's death reached our ears in that house, too. It had been months since we'd talked—barely more than a few messages here and there since he'd visited my house that night when Nim had one of her big lottery dreams. For all its ghosts and pictures of skeletal monks, living in Chiang Mai can make you forget that people die, that another day isn't guaranteed. For the expats, death becomes another one of those country-specific nuisances, like speeding tickets or expensive massages, that you simply leave behind when you come here.

I was shocked to hear Gabe was gone. He was crazy, but he was *good people*, too. Garrett and Peach had found out about Gabe through a realtor who was shopping his house in Samoeng at a low price. I furrowed my brow—*hadn't I heard from him recently?*

"Here," Garrett offered. "Peach is about to get on the phone with the realtor now. We can ask for you."

We both gave Hop a look and he slunk off to another room, mumbling something in the northern dialect that I didn't catch. Peach put the call on speakerphone so we could eavesdrop. Garrett always went out of his way to translate although our level of fluency was more or less even, which at times annoyed me. Nice guys are easier to forgive, though. It was now close to the holiday season—I was expecting to hear that Gabe had passed away earlier in December. He really looked to be in good health when I saw him last. The conversation followed its typical course. Finally, Peach got to the question, and the answer came. Garrett and I looked at each other blankly: both of us were bad with the names of months.

"August. They say he died in August, from a stroke."

August?

"*Mai, mai, mai*," I said, sensing a mix-up. "He came to my house in September. That's definitely not right."

This time, however, there was no mistranslation. The realtor even informed Peach that he had gotten there in time to see paramedics carting Gabe into an ambulance. He had kept Gabe's black cane as a memento; it was laying on the front porch where the ex-cop had taken his final fall—*my, my, my.*

I looked at Hop with my mouth agape. Through the sliding doors I could see the ceiling lights flashing around him, but he wasn't paying them any mind. I went inside and we sat down together, stunned, attempting to process yet another impossibility. Could we be getting *our* dates wrong? But that wasn't the case. I had just gotten a visa extension a few days prior to seeing Gabe, and my passport was stamped for early September. Hop recalled reading the story about the pig born with extra toes around that time, too. But—*how?* I had touched him. He was *there*. I'd always thought spirits were made of stuff like clouds, but this man had appeared at my house in the flesh. My hands were shaking.

Hop's head bowed in disbelief. "We smoked ganja together, man, how could this be…? And I remember his black car."

"And he was complaining about the traffic, remember?"

"*Chai, chai*," replied Hop, stroking his chin as if he no longer noticed the eerie flashing of the salt lamps next to him.

I gave a long sigh, searching my pockets for a lighter. "You remember when life was still normal, bro?"

"Hmm," Hop said, running his hand through his hair. "It seems like life will never be what we think. Always some kind *surprise* for humans." He took a deep pull of the fresh-rolled spliff. "That's why the Buddha told my people: cannot know the knowledge of the world—you can only know with yourself."

"What do you think the Buddha would do in this situation?"

A look of bemusement came over Hop's face. "I think the Buddha won't think about it so much."

"But why did Gabe visit us that night, I mean…?"

"Your girlfriend had the lottery dream that night, *chai mai*?"

"My girlfriend had the lottery dream that night," I repeated, my eyes fixed on Hop.

"Maybe he come to tell you," Hop shrugged. "Maybe P Gabe was same-same as the gods I met in the record shop."

"Damn," I said, looking up at the flickering ceiling light. "You're not a ghost, are you, Hop?"

"If I was dead," Hop grinned, "I would tell you, Prism. *Sure*."

That night I lay awake in bed picturing the lines of Gabe's face, the rasp of his voice, the faintly sour odor of his breath—all the physical ways I had experienced him that evening at my house. Each of us had seen Gabe sitting there, slightly cranky, going on about drug dealers, prostitutes, politics. I'd heard people say *dead men tell no tales* but now we had evidence to the contrary.

And if it was possible for ghosts to be in physical form, why hadn't Mom come by for a visit? Why were dreams the only venue for her warm embrace? I was beginning to fade. I heard a voice dancing through my mind: "Every cloud an omen, every face a memory." Was this thought my own, or had I received it, or was it something recalled…

I found myself running through the narrow streets of a Thai city, weaving through tuk-tuks and the rabble of food stalls and shopfronts, looking for the person I was supposed to meet amid the ageless din of another Asian dusk. There, at the corner, a green figure. The little blue-eyed girl had told me this person would be waiting for me. I was to give them something, something important.

My fingers felt for it in my right pocket—some kind of gift box. I tapped the figure in green on the shoulder, and slowly she turned to me. I was looking into the forgotten face of an old lady who had cared for me as a child, a friend of my mother. She had long since passed.

Confused, I looked at the blur of Thai buyers and sellers around us, the flash of their clothing in the evening's spreading shadows, then back to her face. *My babysitter couldn't be in Lampang.* And then, I was free: it occurred to me that none of this was real. As if my realization itself was a password, the motion of the scene froze, then disintegrated in front of me.

I was in my physical body again, or what appeared to be my physical body. Sunlight was slanting through a gap in the red curtains, and the coolness of the floor pressed against my bare feet. Little slippers were lined up at the door. I was awake, and that much couldn't be questioned.

Another part of me, somewhere, was still asleep, but this here-and-now was elsewhere. I was in a place of business, a lobby with orange and magenta walls, scented with rich oils. Turning around, I found myself at the base of a staircase, and to my right was a painting of a dragonfly perched at the tip of a lotus petal against a lavender sky. It was the kind of art typical to Thai massage parlors. I raised my hand and felt the roughness of the dried paint against my fingers.

"You must help her complete the circle of merit." The voice was so soft that it barely separated from the shop's silence. I looked to the top of the staircase with a start.

I couldn't recognize her at first. She was someone I knew well, hiding behind a veil of déjà vu. But then I really *saw* her. It was the Thai librarian, just not as I'd ever known her before. Her hair was laying down to her bosom, giving her eyes a more vulnerable expression. There was no stiff uniform. She was in a silken pink robe that both matched and clashed with the color of the walls.

"She is waiting for you," the librarian said, looking upward.

I began walking up the stairs, ambivalent...

CHAPTER TWELVE

The librarian kept looking back at me with suspicion as we climbed the narrow stairs. Maybe she thought I would disappear. I could already feel my lucidity unraveling at its fringes, threatening to evaporate. Determined, I focused on the threaded text on the librarian's back: *S. is for Sawadee.*

I muttered the phrase to myself as we gained the second floor. The carpeted stairs gave way to creaking panels of teakwood along a long corridor, and I turned briefly to examine the profile of an indifferent security guard standing in a doorway. We passed countless doors. Sometimes, I fancied that I heard muffled conversations from inside the rooms. It was impossible to investigate—the librarian was walking at a rapid trot. Looking down, I saw that I was floating several inches off the floor. I thought about reaching for my phone to document the feat. No chance: the librarian snapped her fingers with a schoolmaster's impatience. *"Bah!"*

We came upon a small nightstand with a glass vase containing a single rose. I was crushed with a sense of foreboding and halted, but the librarian took my hand. This was our room. A burning odor filled my nostrils, and again I was filled with dread.

My awareness flickered, and I thought I might lose the dream, but my guide yanked me through the doorway, treating me to a new image. We were in a windowless room with a patterned mattress at the center, surrounded by silken pink curtains. On the bed, her head propped up on a cushion, was Nim. She was unconscious. The little night slip she had on was barely enough to cover her ample thighs. My instinct was to put a blanket over her, but the librarian motioned me to stay still.

Candles suddenly illuminated the rustic sconces on the wall. Wisps of black smoke began forming from the floor like serpents. There were three of them. They stabilized into three shadows standing at the foot of the mattress. Each one pulsated with veins of electricity. I wrinkled my nose at the burning smell.

Nim gasped, then let out a small moan, her eyes still closed. There was a whooshing sound. Some kind of circulating current of sparks appeared between the shadows and my supine girlfriend. They were drawing something from her.

I turned to the librarian, who was already watching me with interest. "You don't have much time here," she said in perfect English. "They are hacking her light codes. They will limit the expression of her *Om* frequency and disrupt the timeline, you see?" I felt faint; the librarian yanked my hand again, reattaching me to the dream. "Wake her up, Prism. You must wake her up with a memory."

My normal catalog of memories wasn't available to my dream brain, or they hovered just out of reach, like elusive cats. "NIM," I yelled, "IT'S PRISM!"

One of the shadows turned in my direction, and a force instantly flung me back against the wall, slamming my skull into spinning stars. The pain was physical, and I let out a curse.

"Try, *try*," implored the librarian, kneeling over me. "A memory of love will bring her to life."

159

I looked at Nim again—her body was almost lifted off the mattress, one of her limbs quivering. *Fuck...*

"Neville Longbottom, Ashley Banks, Doi Mae Salong," I shouted at the top of my lungs, embarrassed. Nim's head gave a slight stir. The librarian egged me on. *"Neville Longbottom, Ashley Banks, Doi Mae Salong,"* I repeated with resolve.

The shadows gave a shudder, and their electric pulses gave out. They shriveled into fingers of smoke that crept back into the floorboards. Nim's chest was heaving. Her hands instinctively tried to pull the slip farther down her bare thighs, and she let out confused whimpers.

I got to my feet, rubbing my head. Nim's eyes shot open, and our gazes locked—then everything disappeared and I found myself lying in darkness, drenched in sweat. I shot up and fumbled for the light switch. There was no librarian or massage parlor. Just like that, I was back in Garrett's spare bedroom and it was 3:36 in the morning.

I groaned first in disbelief, then in pain: the back of my head hurt no less than it had in the dream. (If you can even call it that.) Something the librarian had said still danced in my mind. *"The Om frequency..."*

I went downstairs and turned on the coffee maker, feeling impatient for daylight. The desperation in Nim's eyes haunted me. Brooding over black coffee, my thoughts turned to my mother, and I didn't sleep for the rest of the night.

At last, morning came. Hop had announced that he was swearing off tobacco for our trip, but this was quickly proven a caprice on his part. He succumbed as the Volkswagen snaked through emerald provinces and the sweet air of thick forests poured in through our windows.

We decided to skip Lampang and head straight for Phayao,

assuming that Nim had already performed merit in the former city and only needed to discover Wat Luang Ratcha to complete her circle. Phayao is a five-hour drive from Garrett's place in Mae Rim—we set out before the curtain of morning fog had lifted from the mountains. It was December, and the air was polished with a glossy chill at sunrise. By 10 a.m., of course, the heat always prevailed.

We'd loaded all of Hop's reggae and Molam records back into the van, and Garrett had donated a record player that we could plug into the dash with an adapter. With Hop manning the van, volume wouldn't be an issue. It sounded like we had some damn 808s in the back. *Were fugitives supposed to be this loud?*

Somewhere in the bedlam of that last week, Open Source had sent me the final version of our Chiang Mai song, modeled after Quik's "Rosecrans" cut. I'd listened to it in headphones about ten times, vacillating between disappointment and elation. That's how it is when I hear a Prism song for the first time. It's impossible for a lyricist to separate himself from his influences, to listen to his own voice from an objective distance, or to hear it as something unique in the universe. At least not at first. Then, usually, something strange happens: you stop hearing the voice on the record as your own, and you start referring to the recording as if it was someone else who made it. You talk about yourself in the third person like Rickey Henderson, at times glowingly. Sometimes it feels like Prism is merely an artist whose work I follow closely.

Everything on this track was clean, tight. It didn't have that same infectious *bump* as the Quik song, but that's splitting hairs— our song was really good. Open Source sounded like a millennial Grand Puba with his upbeat, sing-song patterns, matching my monotone rhyme acrobatics, keeping everything loose. I noticed that he'd reinserted the sample where the trumpets came in, stuttering the delivery so it went *"s-s-sombat, sombat"* to stay in time with the beat. Concept would mess with this, I thought to myself with a smile. I wanted to see how the song sounded with those alien acoustics. On went Suga Free's "Doe Doe and a Skunk" to get Hop back in the hip-hop zone.

"Make me want to smoke again, man," he said halfway through, swaying his head emotively like someone at a techno festival.

"Quik sampled 'Loose Ends' for this," I laughed. "You like it?"

"Feel like we're going to the *outer* space. What song is it?"

"The sample? I think 'Nights of Pleasure.' "

Hop nodded cheerfully and poked the air with "yo, yo" fingers. The opening synths of our song arrived and paused Hop's performance. His whole van started humming with bass as the keys cascaded like cerulean rivulets, Source's voice sailing over the top. All of the elements were perfectly fused under Hop's influence (the song was still unmixed). Where the trumpets were grayscale before, they now exuded bright, electric hues. *It's kind of funny how one pencil can scramble timelines…*

"You guys use Thai sample, right?" asked Hop as we listened to the closing notes.

"Yeah," I said excitedly, "you know it?"

"Man, I think I heard it before. Like a Molam record, *chai mai…*"

"Yeah, Source didn't know where it was from."

"*Sombat, sombat.* I have an idea, maybe I'll show you later."

Hop took an exit off the two-lane highway to fill up on some gas. We were about halfway between Chiang Mai and Phayao. I got out, yawned, and ambled over to the urinals, which were situated on the edge of a gaping rice field whose green filled the land to its horizon.

This little road trip was completely on faith. Who really knew where Nim was? I hadn't spoken to her since that one day at Garrett's house. I didn't know anything anymore. After the thing with Gabe, I felt suspicious of solidity in general. The pure air of the rice field in my lungs was the only thing I couldn't doubt.

I checked for updates on the lottery scandal. Now they were saying that the only solution was to overhaul the entire Thai lottery system. Starting next year, according to the *Bangkok Courier*, the lottery would go completely paperless—instead of buying tickets, people would have to download an app with a biometric login, at which point they would automatically receive random numbers twice a month. According to officials, this was the only way to defeat government corruption. This app, they claimed, had just been "thrown together" in the last week. *Weird.* Sometimes it feels like the future is a circus requiring that you become a robot to gain entry. Or will it…?

We were back on the road, knifing around curves on switchbacks. The functionality of Hop's van didn't seem too affected by its driver's EMF charge, outside of the fact that the needles on the odometer were constantly spinning back and forth, making us unsure of how much gas we had or how fast we were going. The tangle of Buddha amulets rattled and swayed with each curve, and I began to zone out. Presently, Hop lit a new joint and motioned for me to find a particular song on his phone.

"Prism, you hear about the *tab lang*[149] stones now returning to *prathet Thai*[150]? *Kuy dai yen mai*[151]?"

I hadn't.

"I think you should know," he said, watching the froths of

---

[149] *Tab lang:* Votive stones for Lord Vishnu (ทับหลัง)

[150] *Prathet Thai:* The country of Thailand (ประเทศไทย)

[151] *Kuy dai yen mai:* "Have you heard?" (เคยได้ยินไหม)

smoke trail out of his window. "The *tab lang* stones are important for Thai people. They show *Phra Narai*[152], you know? Many years ago, someone steal them. *Tab lang hai*[153]. You know where they go?"

I didn't.

"Museum in America. It was a big, big scandal. Stolen artifacts. And around that time, Michael Jackson came to Thailand."

"Michael Jackson?"

"Yep. Big concert in *Khrungtep*. Many people go to see Michael Jackson. But after the show was finished, many people complain that the grass was damaged by special effect, *koh jai mai?*"

"This was after the *Dangerous* album, right?" I quipped.

"*Chai*, dangerous *mak*[154]. So the Thai band Carabao made a song for this situation. 'Tab Lang.' I'll play it for you…"

A zany electric guitar pulsated through the van, followed by a strident male voice that made imprecations against the US government for the Vietnam War, theft of the *tab lang* artifacts, and the imposition of global pop stars that were irrelevant to Thai culture. It was a rousing anthem draped in the sonic fog of early '90s recordings. Hop chimed in on every end rhyme and belted out the chorus, which called for Michael Jackson to beat it and the *tab lang* artifacts to be returned.

"I've never heard a Michael Jackson diss record before," I said as the song ended, laughing at Hop's enthusiasm.

"The *tab lang* they talk about," he replied solemnly, "is a holy stone of the gods. I think it's the same as the *silajaruk*."

"Aren't they different?"

"Normally, yes. The *silajaruk* was used in old days to make

---

[152] *Phra Narai:* Lord Vishnu (พระนารายณ์)

[153] *Tab lang hai:* "The stones disappeared." (ทับหลังหาย)

[154] *Mak:* Very (มาก)

announcements by local administration. They also made the *duang chata* the horoscope to show the time. But now I think about what Lanna and Malila say to us…"

"They're magic stones that create portals between timelines, right?"

"So maybe there's a battle for the *tab lang* stones for this reason. It's not just to show in Chicago museum, *chai mai*. The stones have special power. But many of them disappear…"

"And we have to make new ones, somehow."

"*Aow Phra Narai kun ma*[155]!"

Hop and I communed in silence for the rest of the trip. The sky grew overcast as we advanced toward Phayao; raindrops would intermittently splatter the windshield. The mountaintops dominating the highway were wreathed in clouds.

I continued my research on Gabe's case—I'd tried in vain to find an obituary, which didn't seem to exist in either English or Thai. Eventually, I stumbled across a post made in a Vietnam Veterans message board from years ago by someone named "GabeMan" living in Chiang Mai. I couldn't recall Gabe talking about military stuff, but it *sounded* like him. The poster mentioned that he'd been stationed at the Nakhon Phanom air base on the Mekong River, working as a pilot in the 56th Special Operations Wing. His missions were top secret and "technically," he said, "we didn't exist."

The poster claimed that his exposure to Agent Orange was responsible for his heart disease and different skin conditions, but that the VA refused to compensate him after the war. I vaguely remembered noticing splotches of discoloration on Gabe's wrists and neck. There were things he witnessed in Nakhon Phanom, he

---

[155] *Aow Phra Narai kun ma:* "Bring back Lord Vishnu." (เอาพระนารายณ์คืนมา)

said, that he would take to his grave. He also made some curious remarks about a "spiritual awakening" he'd had during the war. There were "other people, different classes of agents" at the base who were trying to steer the war in a different direction. Some of these people were "very wise" and had, according to the poster, proven to him that he had experienced past lives as a Thai person. Many of his statements were incoherent and allusive.

Arriving in the town of Phayao is an anticlimactic affair. Signs of settlement and business begin to appear on either side, little pharmacies and the women under the parasols with their *huay* tickets spread out on tables in front of them. You go through a couple of traffic lights, expecting that soon you'll arrive in the center. Then you look up and realize you're already on your way out of town, surrounded again by the oblivion of the countryside. The town ends at its beginning.

Exhausted, we finally checked into a hotel outside of Wat Sikom Kam, located on the shores of the town's giant lake that mirrors the peaks of Doi Bussaracum. It was my first time in Phayao, and it's likely that it was also my last. Few outsiders ever return to Phayao. It's a dream of the northern Thai valleys that is better suited as an emanation from the vents of memory, something that induces a feeling rather than calling you to experience it again.

Leaving Hop in the room, I decided to go for a walk, wondering if I'd see Nim. I passed under the reflective street signs that curved up bronzely at the corners, my legs keeping pace with my wandering mind in the brisk twilight. I started to write a short essay in my thoughts, which went something like this:

The noodle soup lady makes me feel like a son—notice how I left out the possessive pronoun. Sometimes I don't feel like anyone's son anymore. Around her, I am a son. She's an aging woman from the south whose youth still blooms in her face. It's not any pronounced or deliberate action on her part that gives me this feeling. She's a busybody—always stirring the vats, slicing parsley, but without a touch of worry or haste. Her smile is effortlessly maternal. Mostly quiet in her work, she only chides the cats when they meow. The entire place would collapse into dust if she left. That could never happen. She asks me how I want my eggs as if she's asked me every morning. The order complete, I sit down to wait, and in doing so I seat myself in the aura of her activity, an ageless trust washing over me. I don't know her name, she doesn't know mine. Her care meets me in the place I feel empty, and her noodles are thicker than passionfruit vines.

I stuffed my hands into my jacket against the night's light chill as the streetlights blinked on. The sidewalks were eerily quiet. There was a shopfront that came into focus on the other side of the street.

In the window was a mannequin wearing a yellow dress, and standing in front of the window was a lone figure in green. It was a woman in denim shorts and a tight hoodie whose legs I recognized. When she turned to look at me, I saw she was bald, and I became gripped by confusion. Her eyebrows shot up, and she called out to me in a voice that was accustomed to cradling my name. I jumped across the street and we embraced. It was Nim's first time in Phayao, too.

FORM F

Before I saw S. for the last time, she told me many things. She knew it was possible that she could become trapped in the future. I have every reason, by the way, to believe that her concerns came true. S. told me that her people were not from the sky, but from a realm within our earth. They are called the Jahnavid, or "people of knowledge." Their kingdom is rich in meadows, lakes, forests, and crystal caves. At different times in the past, the Jahnavid have entered our realm to live alongside us. They have influenced our fields of philosophy, healing, music, and physics. Their people of learning are in the same class as royalty. S. described her race to me as "students and defenders of natural law." The Jahnavid are fiercely independent. They believe that freedom is impossible without bravery. Their symbols left in our world speak to us in ways we aren't aware of, and it is better this way. Some of their messages are shown through animals. They have allied with beings in other dimensions, too. Making sure not to interfere in our growth is very important to them, S. explained. Their principles of non-interference were revised when certain prophecies of their priests started to come true, and they saw that their fate was linked to ours. Disasters started occurring in their world; their traditions of succession were upset. They awoke to their battle with the Archons and became adept at maneuvering across timelines to form resistance. The Jahnavid organized the White Elephants themselves. The people on the street awakened by rose petals were secretly trained at

Nakhon Phanom to become diplomats or other positions of political skill. One man that I located became an adviser to the king of Bhutan. But this is not the only way the Jahnavid have chosen to influence us. They decided that there was no choice but to crossbreed with humans so that our path to mastery was shorter. The Jahnavid halflings are not so different in appearance from normal humans. Their character is bubbly and creative, but they are known to prefer being outsiders and are sometimes viewed as stubborn. The halflings have intense relationships with their human parents. This relationship can continue in many forms. Wan Wan was a Jahnavid halfling who was taken from her Burmese mother, S. told me. It was certain that the mother had been reached by Wan Wan in the dream world after her death at Nakhon Phanom. The bond between a human parent and their halfling continues to grow after death intercedes. The parent learns that their child was assigned to them as a teacher. I believe that Wan Wan was assigned to me as a t

(incomplete)

CHAPTER THIRTEEN

The reports that Malila was dead were retracted almost as soon as they were released. A new picture of her drinking a *Chang*[156] beer led Thai people to ask how her social media accounts were posthumously active. Now it was said that she was "missing," which was hardly any sort of update from the weeks before. An opinion column appeared in the *Courier* that questioned Malila's very existence, speculating that she had always been a composite character played by several actors. Anyway, the column went on, catching a person named Malila wasn't the important thing; the Thai government should instead prioritize a digital lottery system in which everyone's numbers were attached to their identity. It was their "social and civic responsibility" to do so, the writer claimed.

The false news of Malila's demise didn't sit well with Nim. She had been trailed by a black car as she went from temple to temple in Lampang. Another vehicle of similar appearance had been parked outside her hotel since she arrived in Phayao. Nim had shaved her head to look like an unassuming nun, avoiding the glamour that she normally flaunted. She looked a little like Chow

---

[156] *Chang*: Elephant (ช้าง)

Yun-fat's character in *Crouching Tiger, Hidden Dragon*. I didn't tell her this.

Nim's experience of donating to the old temples as a national fugitive had made her haughty and distant. In retrospect, I can see that she had lost interest in the mystery of our pursuit and was in Phayao merely to go through those final motions out of obligation, out of a tepid sense of honor. Nim was stripped of her lottery glow. Our lone hug that evening was the only time she showed any atavistically romantic feelings for me. Still, I don't blame Nim for what she did in Phayao. Not at all.

She was unfazed, even terse when I told her the news about Gabe. "All the old stories are true," she said with a shrug.

It was hard to know how much Nim knew at that point. There were most likely many things she wasn't telling me. She did mention that the lottery man had visited her one more time in the real world. He sat with one leg crossed over the other in slacks on a chair near her bed one night, counseling Nim on Buddhist ethics, complimenting her decisions. Everything would work out, he assured her. The next morning, she found his cane resting on her bedside table. Her door, of course, had remained locked the entire night. I wondered if that was the same night I had rescued her with the librarian in the dream world. Real or not, the back of my head was still sore from being thrown against that damn wall.

The only thing that seemed to give Nim any cheer was Hop's presence, which had come as a surprise to her. She probably hadn't understood why the two of us were together back at Garrett's house. When Nim heard Hop retell his racy adventures in Chinatown, she permitted herself a hearty laugh.

"Hop, you wear condom or not?" she prodded after Hop explained his tryst with Lanna in the back of the record shop.

"*Mai dai aow ma, krub, ga luy mai sai luy*[157]," replied Hop, grinning ear to ear and a little red in the face. "Should be daddy to alien now."

"*Ow!*" cried Nim in a show of faux disapproval. Her laughter bubbled forth as it had the night she was drunk at Topic 36.

A day later, we set out to find Wat Luang Ratcha, the temple that no longer existed, without much of a plan. Nim had located the place where it once stood on an old map. That was all we had. We needed to drive east along a two-lane road hemmed in by dripping thickets of forest. It was morning. The sky was a blank gray, and fog still clung to the mountaintops, looming over the lake.

The three of us piled into Hop's faithful old van, which miraculously survived everything described in this account. Nim muttered complaints as she shoved aside Hop's stacks of old records in the back seat. I had asked her about the purpose of bringing a Gucci duffle bag, but she evaded my questions. Her bright-red lipstick looked almost opulent compared to her white hoodie and gray sweatpants. She had also put on a startling blond wig—something I have no choice but to remember vividly.

Still bleary-eyed after our first cup of coffee, Nim and I were surprised to find ourselves being driven up to the police station. We looked at Hop in alarm. He was fumbling with his phone to switch off the blaring reggae music, which had already attracted the nearest officer on duty. We must have been quite a sight to this guy. Nim reached up and shook Hop's shoulder urgently, cursing in Thai.

"He can be the escort for us," Hop explained to me in a loud voice. "We don't know what can happen..."

---

[157] *Mai dai aow ma, krub, ga luy mai sai luy:* "Never brought it, never wore it." (ไม่ได้เอามาครับก็เลยไม่ใสเลย)

I turned around to look at Nim, who had fallen quiet. Hop was already negotiating with the Phayao officer, informing him that someone was following us around, possibly with bad intentions. We needed an officer to stay with us as we visited some of the local *wats*[158]. He leaned in the window to peer at us. After some more back-and-forth, the cop's demeanor became accommodating.

Hop advised me to give the man a tip. I fished out a few thousand *baht* and handed it over with a brisk *khob khun*[159] *krub*. We were making a huge gamble, mainly because we had no idea what was about to happen, and there was a possibility that our own activity would be deemed the most suspicious. Besides, how did we know that some provinces *weren't* taking the search for Nim and Malila seriously? I gave Nim another questioning look, but she only gave me a pacifying blink and nod. I was the *farang*, what did I know?

We made a pretense of visiting some of the temples around town, even getting out and taking pictures of the candlelit statues at Wat Li. Nim hurried us along impatiently. There wasn't much time, she insisted.

I coaxed Hop into playing some old Carlos Santana to calm our nerves. There's never been a time when I was happy about a squad car being right behind me. Hop tried to engage Nim about her trip to Lampang. Stonily gazing out the window, she mostly replied with little throat noises, and soon Hop abandoned his attempts.

Everything seemed exceptionally still outside. The birds had been silent all morning. Even the age-old oak trees, cloudy with moss, seemed barren of life. As we came up on Wat Sikhom Kham, another car appeared behind the cop. It was black and moving fast.

---

[158] *Wats:* Temples (วัด)

[159] *Khob khun:* "Thank you." (ขอบคุณ)

Looking back, Nim implored Hop to go faster. The cop started flashing his lights as the black car overtook him. Hop's VW lagged, barely capable of anything beyond 100 kilometers an hour. It was built for joy rides, not car chases.

Now another black car appeared behind the cop. We rounded a curve—then Hop slammed hard on the brakes. Our little caravan had company. Surrounding us were massive creatures with flapping ears and long, drooping trunks, being guided by small Thai men with bandannas tied on their heads. We had joined the ranks of a lumbering troupe of elephants and their mahouts.

A narrow path opened in front of us and immediately closed behind us. There must have been at least twenty of them, maybe more. The creatures all merged into one continental organism, pressing in on us from all sides, examining us neutrally as we passed through its calloused tunnel of trunks, carrying us with an ancient momentum. The mouth of the tunnel opened wider, and we finally broke through.

Looking back, the herd of elephants was like an eclipse moving at the speed of molasses. It was the last we saw of any of the vehicles behind us. Hop shouted exultantly and punched the air outside of his window.

"Talok[160] *sha-bing,"* blond Nim commented with a sigh.

We hadn't been driving for long when we saw a hitchhiker on the side of the road. As we got closer, we could see that the man was beckoning us to pull over. He looked very familiar, which is more than you can say for most faceless people.

"It's him, it's him," Nim said urgently. "Open the door."

I did so, then wriggled my way into the back seat to let the man sit in the front. He climbed in gingerly, setting his cane down on

---

[160] *Talok:* Funny (ตลก)

the floor first. The man was solid, but I could see his body was rimmed in a kind of dull light, and in a seated position he was actually floating several inches off the chair.

Hop shot us a nervous glance. "*Pai nai*[161], *krub?*"

The man answered like a well-read tourist: "*Pai Wat Luang Ratcha*[162]." I looked at Nim with my mouth open, but she only hushed me, putting one finger to her lips. I felt a chill that outlined every vein and artery in my body. *King Naresuan?*

Briefly, we were four. As I studied the apparition in front of us, resisting the urge to touch its sleeved arm, we saw a white Lexus SUV parked ahead on the shoulder, rear lights flashing. It all happened too fast.

Nim was leaning forward and telling Hop to pull over. She turned to me and planted a deep kiss on my lips. "Goodbye, Prism."

We came to a stop, and Nim hopped out with her duffel bag. Frozen, I watched her backside disappear as she slid into the white SUV and pulled the door shut behind her. The vehicle peeled off and disappeared around the bend, and that was that—my lottery queen was gone.

Days later, she called from Tokyo to tell me she was on her way to Hong Kong. She reminded me that it had been Suphankanlaya's fate to live outside of the Thai Kingdom, too. Anyhow, the five percent from Nim's lottery winnings was already yielding her profit in stocks. All of her blessings are inevitable, imperial.

"She doesn't like my van?"

"Hop, she's gone, man."

---

[161] *Pai nai:* "Where are you going?" (ไปไหน)

[162] *Pai Wat Luang Ratcha:* "I'm going to Wat Luang Ratcha." (ไปวัดหลวงราช)

"Ahhhhh...*jing lor*[163] *krub?*"

"*Jing jing.*"

We both looked at the figure in the front seat. He was raising a single bony finger as if to say, *"Onward."* My heart was pounding. Nim's Chanel was still filling the van's interior, punctuating her absence.

We lurched forward again. Every time I looked at the hitch-hiker, I had to do a double-take because there was something different about him. His appearance was becoming more detailed. I was now looking at an older white man with a ring of stubble on a bald head, big ears, tangled eyebrows, and lines deeper than tree rings on his face. I was looking at *Gabe.*

"Prism," Hop said, "turn on your DJ Quik song, man." I could hear in his voice that Hop had recognized our hitchhiker, too.

"You never told me what the sample is. Do we have it back here?" I asked, rummaging through a colorful collage of vinyl.

"Look for the title, uh, *na ti dek. Na ti dek*[164]. Could be a yellow cover, *mong*[165]..."

We were nearing the site of the temple. Source's punchy Chiang Mai groove again vibrated through the van's metal spine, only this time it was louder. I don't know how Hop pulled that off. He quickly affixed a number of shungite magnets to the front windshield, reaching out with his right hand as he held the wheel with his left. Ahead of us was a pit of blackness—Hop's timing couldn't have been more perfect.

Closer, we could make out three pillars of smoke. They were growing taller, ribbed with electric pulsations. I knew they'd be

---

[163] *Jing lor:* "Really?" (จริงเหรอ)

[164] *Na ti dek:* "A Child's Duty" (หน้าที่เด็ก)

[165] *Mong:* Maybe (มั้ง)

waiting for us. The volume of my verse heightened by several decibels and Hop floored it, heading straight for the blinking columns of vapor.

There was a moment where I thought we would make it cleanly, then a moment I thought we'd die. The reality ended up being somewhere in between. We were cast into a tailspin, then blown off the road by what felt like an explosion. The poor van had landed in the shrubbery but just short of the tree line.

Hop and I looked up—the three columns of smoke were collapsing, flaring out like mushroom clouds and engulfing the road. Suddenly, the smoke coalesced into a point and took the shape of a triangle craft, which shot upward with a *whoosh* and vanished. Some residual smoke draped itself across the tree limbs.

"For Lanna," Hop shouted, raising two fists in the air.

"The girl, or the kingdom?"

"Yes."

"Wh—never mind. Is this the album?"

"Let's me see," Hop replied, taking a yellow-sleeved record from my hand. "Ah, *chai luy!*"

"Also, are we stuck here?"

"I think we need a UFO," grumbled Hop.

He turned the key in the ignition and the engine sputtered, failed, and sputtered again. Dead as dungarees. But after a minute, Hop somehow had the thing purring again, and we finally rumbled out of the grass, reborn.

The apparition of Gabe, which had remained stoic for the whole episode, again lifted a single bony finger: *Onward.* A shaft of sunlight sliced across the road and dappled the edge of the forest floor with flickering shadows of bamboo leaves.

We drove for several minutes without incident, then pulled up to a clearing on our right, marked by a sign and the scrambled ruins of brick foundations, buried in leaves and moss.

"Wat Luang Ratcha," Hop confirmed, leaning out of his window to read the sign.

"Gabe," I said. "*Gabe*, is that you?"

The apparition stirred, raising its hands in a *wai* and bowing its head. "*Pai Wat Luang Ratcha.*" The gravelly voice wasn't Gabe's, but reverberated from the depths of another era. Hop and I exchanged a look.

"Are we doing this?" I asked.

"*Tom dai luy krub*[166]." Hop turned his head toward the apparition and returned the *wai*.

"What's the story of this song?"

"Hmm...I want to know how Source got this Thai sample. This song very old, na. It's about the ten things to be a good child of *prathet Thai*. Not so interesting for me. But it's the only recording for this singer. They say she was a *ma du...beb*[167], the person healing with magic."

Of course.

I removed the vinyl from its sleeve, fiddled at Garret's record player 'til it was resurrected, then set the needle on...it was a jaunty 1930s recording with a full horn line, almost jarring you with its dated optimism.

"*Sombat chat tang rak sa*[168]!" My friend amplified the song so loudly that it sounded like three megaphones were attached to the roof of the van.

The apparition removed itself from the vehicle and began walking toward the ruins. Its movement was only a rippling distortion

---

[166] *Tom dai luy krub:* "We can do this." (ทำได้เลยครับ)

[167] *Beb:* "Like…" (แบบ)

[168] *Sombat chat tang rak sa:* "National treasures must be preserved!" (สมบัติชาติต้องรักษา)

in the scenery. We got out too.

Something was happening—at first I thought something was wrong with the record. The song had caught on one of the singer's high notes, which had isolated itself fairylike in the air, and this single note was issuing forth as a hypnotic vibrato.

Hop yanked my sleeve and I looked up. A vast grid of twinkling lines was forming in the clearing in front of us.

The key to the temple is the key that it's in.

A tiered roof took shape, the lines tracing a pair of curled eaves on either side, and the magnetic pillars of a portico came into view at the center. A staircase led up to a spectral doorway that now swung open.

The vibrato note had reached such a velocity that it seemed to fill all the forests of Phayao, then it began to shift into a flat, hollow tone that met our ears like a piercing whistle. The apparition was slowly approaching the staircase. No longer in the form of Gabe, King Naresuan was now adorned in a snow-white Nehru jacket and soaring gold crown. As he mounted the stairs, the piercing tone gradually shifted into the chanting of a hundred monks, dropping lower and lower. *The Om frequency.*

In front of us, we could see a shimmering iridescent *viharn*, burning so brightly with jewels that we feared for our eyes. Its lines still trembled like a spiderweb in the wind. Seven pagodas had formed around the viharn like orbiting moons.

As King Naresuan reached the threshold, the two of us staggered backward. Wat Luang Ratcha began flashing countless colors at multiple frames per second...*oh! oh!* We turned our faces against the blinding white light; it filled our limbs and rendered us weightless, free.

...When I came to, I was lifting myself from the ground, squinting my eyes against the sunlight refracting through the towering glass pagodas that rose around me. Someone was calling me by my birth name. I looked and saw two human shapes near a six-foot stone with lines of script radiating from its surface. I approached them and saw them for who they were. One was the librarian—whom I now know as *S.*—and the other was a little girl with shining blue eyes. Her laughter greeted me like the sound of a running brook. Within her little face was written the promise of everything I had loved about her, poised in parturiency.

S. gave the girl a nudge, and a sheaf of papers was passed from her small hand to mine. On the back of one of the pages were the beginnings of a tiger butterfly drawn in crayon.

"Here," she giggled, "you can finish it for me."

A rose-colored gift box was placed in my hands. When I looked up again, I saw an image of my mother as I had known her, bathed in white light and cradling a baby in her arms. The *silajaruk* stone was now shining brighter than the glass pagodas. Around her was a circle of humanlike beings whose spirits throbbed with joy. I watched the memories awaken and rise like doves at dawn. What made those beings different, I saw, was the same as the parts of me I never understood.

At last, we have reached the starting point of my composition. When I turned over the sheaf of papers, the heading read *Form A*, and that was how I learned the true tale of Malila. Nim helped to translate the documents from abroad—no one deserved the task more than her. She told me that Form E was lost, and I still haven't heard what happened to the end of Form F. It is typical of translators to take liberties, of course.

As for the contents of the gift box, the interior was encrusted in crystals and lined with black velvet. I suspect that it was the fanciest delivery of a single pencil in history. That's right, one pencil, with the words *Remember Who You Are* engraved on the side.

This text ensued. I set out to piece everything together like a many-colored money tree, faltering as I strove to master my astonishment. By now, you've figured it out: the writer speaks as a being from one world who finds himself in another. A different fortune surrounds me. If you are reading this, exhale, for your timeline has been corrected, and all is well. Mother, your mission is complete.

About the Author

Born in South Carolina and raised in Virginia, Julian Mihdi is also the author of *Chimera: Four Stories and a Novelette* and the co-author of the novel *Emerald Chant*. He graduated from George Mason University in 2009 and went on to receive a TEFL certificate for teaching English as a second language. Arriving in Southeast Asia as a teacher, Mihdi became steeped in Thai culture by living and working in Chiang Rai, Chiang Mai, and Bangkok over the better part of the last decade. Mihdi enjoys spending his time reading novels, listening to classic hip-hop, practicing Thai, playing basketball, discovering secret cafes, and pursuing the true meaning of NFTs and their place in humanity's future.

Glossary

1. Farang(s): Foreigner (ฝรั่ง)
2. Sapparot: Pineapple (สับปะรด)
3. Sois: Avenues (ซอย)
4. Geng mak mak: "Great job!" (เก่งมาก ๆ)
5. Len huay: "Played the lottery." (เล่นหวย)
6. Na kha: An expression of female politeness (คะ)
7. Chai mai: "Right?" (ใช่ไหม)
8. Hong nam: Bathroom (ห้องน้ำ)
9. Chai: "Yes" (ใช่)
10. Mai chai: "No" (ไม่ใช่)
11. Baht: Thai unit of currency, 30=1 USD at the time of writing (บาท)
12. Check bin: Common phrase for settling a bill (เช็คบิล)
13. Mai wai luy: "I just can't with you!" (ไม่ไหวเลย)
14. Muban: Village/neighborhood (หมู่บ้าน)
15. Puh-un maa laew: "My friend is here." (เพื่อนมาแล้ว)
16. Krub: An expression of male politeness (ครับ)
17. Wai: A universal sign of respect (ไหว้)
18. Mao ri-yung: "Are you drunk yet?" (เมาหรือยัง)
19. Mai tung: "Not quite." (ไม่ถึง)
20. Khon dee: A good person (คนดี)
21. Arrai wa: "What the hell?" (อะไรว้า)
22. Khao soi: Coconut-based soup with egg noodles (ข้าวซอย)
23. Sawadee kha: Standard Thai greeting (สวัสดี)
24. An nang-suh ru-yang kha: "Have you read this book yet?" (อ่านหนังสือหรือยัง)
25. Ah, du dee na kha: "Have a good look." (ดูดี)
26. Pai laew!: "I'm gone!" (ไปแล้ว)
27. Mai tung wa: "It means that…" (หมายถึงว่ะ)

28. Tum mai?: "Why?" (ทำไม)

29. Mai chai luh: "Wasn't he?" (ไม่ไชเหรอ)

30. Nuy jai: "This is frustrating." (เหนื่อยใจ)

31. Mai kin moo: "You don't eat pork." (ไม่กินหมู)

32. Visakha Bucha: Holiday celebrating the birth, death & enlightenment of Gautama Buddha (วันวิสาขบูชา)

33. Mae: Mother (แม่)

34. Pa: Father (พ่อ)

35. Nom Towhu: Soy milk (นมเต้าหู้)

36. Samlor: Old three-wheel taxi (สามล้อ)

37. Luk ban fai: Ball of fire (ลูกบาลไฟ)

38. Ya tum yung ngan: "Stop that!" (อย่าทำอย่างนั้น)

39. Wen gam: "What bad luck!" (เวรกรรม)

40. Manut tang dao: Aliens (มนุษย์ต่างดาว)

41. Mai ben rai, luk: "Don't worry, child." (ไม่เป็นไร ลูก)

42. Yang mai hen arrai luy: "I still can't see anything." (ยังไม่เห็นอะไรเลย)

43. Nang: "Little sister." (น้อง)

44. Somtam: Papaya salad (ส้มตำ)

45. Jok: Thai rice porridge (โจ๊ก)

46. nam prik: Notoriously spicy Thai chili sauce. (น้ำพริก)

47. kuy tiew: Standard Thai noodle soup. (ก๋วยเตี๋ยว)

48. Rotis: Pan-fried bread with condensed milk. (โรตี)

49. Yuu nai nia: "Where are you?" (อยู่ไหนเนี่ย)

50. Jing jing: "For real" (จริงๆ)

51. Khou man kai: Rice and chicken dish (ข้าวมันไก่)

52. Cha tai: Thai tea (ชาไทย)

53. Eee hia!: "Shit!" (อีเหี้ย)

54. Ma du: Witch or prophetess (หมอดู)

55. Rang kai kong chan mai chua fang: "My body disobeyed." (ร่างกายของฉันไม่เชื่อฟัง)

56. Khon purma: Burmese person (คนพม่า)

57. Na song san: Pitiful (น่า สงสาร)

58. P: A title of respect for elders (พี่)

59. Mun ben eek khon: "It's another person." (มันเป็นอีกคน)

60. Luh: Verbal question mark (เหรอ)

61. Chob: "Like" (ชอบ)

62. Hi-so: A colloquial abbreviation of "high society" (ไฮโซ)

63. Yim luy: "So cool!" (ยิ้มเลย)

64. Eek laew: "Again!" (อีกแลว)

65. Oolong: Chinese green tea (อุหลง)

66. Tom ruat: Police (ตำรวจ)

67. Khou ja aow tent pai Chiang Puak tuk khun: "They'll set up tents in Chang Puak every night!" (เขาจะเอาเต็นท์ไปช้างเผือกทุกคืน)

68. Karsai: Traditional form of genital therapy (กษัย)

69. Karsai ben prapani tang sassana: "Karsai is a religious custom." (กษัยเป็นประเพณีทางศาสนา)

70. Hai kan raksa: "Give healing." (ให้การรักษา)

71. Suay mai: "Am I beautiful?" (สวยไหม)

72. Som nam na: A way of mocking a friend's plight (สมน้ำหน้า)

73. Pai nai ma, pai nai ma: "Where have you been?" (ไปไหนมา)

74. Hen kaa kuam ti rao song bai ra blao: "Did you get the message we sent or not?" (เห็นข้อความที่เราส่งไปหรือเปล่า)

75. Kaa kuam arrai: "What message?" (ข้อความอะไร)

76. Hai chan klab ban: "Take me home" (ให้ฉันกลับบ้าน)

77. Prism, glua kun pai: "This is too scary" (กลัวเกินไป)

78. Bah: "Come on" (ปะ)

79. Aow Chang, kuwad yai: "I'll have a big bottle of Chang beer." (เอาช้างขวดใหญ่)

80. Raew: "Hurry up!" (เร็ว)

81. Buad tang mak: Stomach pain (ปวดท้อง)

82. Du menu gan, kha: "Check the menu." (ดูเมนูกัน)

83. Moo ka ta: "Barbecue pork!" (หมูกระทะ)

84. Nam chim suki: Suki sauce (น้ำจิ้มสุกี้)

85. Kod arroi: "Fucking delicious!" (โคตรอร่อย)

86. Dok gulab mai dai me wai puah hi kid, me wai puah hi dom glin tao nan: "Roses aren't for thinking, only smelling." (ดอกกุหลาบไม่ได้มีไว้เพื่อให้คิด มีไว้เพื่อให้ดมกลิ่นเท่านั้น)

87. Chang meng: "Forget it!" (ช่างแม่ง)

88. Mukon nang hen bap nee chai mai…Mukon nang hen bap nee chai mai: "You saw something like this, right?" (เมื่อก่อนน้องเห็นแบบนี้ใช่ไหม)

89. Rao roo tuk yang: "We know everything." (เรารู้ทุกอย่าง)

90. Rao prom hai shuay, kha: "But we are here to help." (แต่เราพร้อมให้ช่วย)

91. Pua kao kid wa chan ben sai lop kong satan tud farang say: "They think I'm a spy at the French embassy." (พวกเขาคิดว่าฉันเป็นสายลับของสถานทูตฝรั่งเศส)

92. Darajak: Galaxy (ดาราจักร)

93. Chang puak: White elephants (ช้างเผือก)

94. Me klin hom mak, chai mai luk: "They smell nice don't they, child?" (มีกลิ่นหอมมากใช่ไหมลูก)

95. Sanuk: Fun, enjoyment (สนุก)

96. Luk chin: Meatballs (ลูกชิ้น)

97. Pad thai: Popular dry noodle dish (ผัดไทย)

98. Sombot: Fortune, treasure (สมบัติ)

99. Ma-kam: Tamarind (มะขาม)

100. Sha-bing: Slang term used to emphasize an adjective. (ฉิบเป๋ง)

101. Tom kha: Coconut-based curry soup. (ต้มข่า)

102. Koh jai mai: "Do you understand?" (เข้าใจไหม)

103. Phra: Title for a king. (พระ)

104. Chedi: Pagoda (เจดีย์)

105. Viharns: Building of worship (วิหาร)

106. Hen mai: "Do you see?" (เห็นไหม)

107. Nippan: Nirvana (นิพพาน)

108. Phra ja attibai noi: The monk will explain. (พระจะอธิบายน่อย)

109. Diew diew: "Hold on." (เดี๋ยวๆ)

110. Mai son jai: "I don't care." (ไม่สนใจ)

111. Duay: Too (ด้วย)

112. Tam sabai sabai: "I took it easy." (ทำสบายๆ)

113. Glua arrai kha: "What are you afraid of?" (กลัวอะไรคะ)

114. Mai tong brien wee-sa: "You don't need to change your visa." (ไม่ต้องเปลี่ยนวีซ่า)

115. Ja bpai kwee kab khon hoi duay kan kha: "We'll go talk with a lottery person together." (จะไปคุยกับคนหวยด้วยกันค่ะ)

116. Kuh karachakan ni: "It's a government officer at…" (คือข้าราชการใน)

117. Bok laew: "(I) told you already!" (บอกแล้ว)

118. Khon kai gu lab: Rose merchant (คนขายกุหลาบ)

119. Kam pood mai oke, dto nan chan mai me reng: "I didn't have the energy to speak." (คำพูดไม่ออกตอนนั้นฉันไม่มีแรง)

120. Jao fa: Local prince (เจ้าฟ้า)

121. Phraya: Ruler (พระยา)

122. Phra kruang: Amulet (พระเครื่อง)

123. kraeng jai: Thai social code of manners and etiquette (เกรงใจ)

124. Chern luy: "Please come in!" (เชิญ)

125. Pad krapow: A rice dish with meat stir-fried in basil. (ผัดกะเพรา)

126. Jao: An expression of politeness native to northern Thailand (เจ้า)

127. Khun: Equivalent to Mr./Ms. (คุณ)

128. Silajaruk: Ceremonial stone historically used to mark official property (ศิลาจารึก)

129. E dok: "Bitch." (อีดอก)

130. Ja tom arrai bong ti rak?: "What are you gonna do, babe?" (จะทำอะไรบ้างที่รัก)

131. Ben shuh khou, tom mai Nim kuan bok Prism: "It's my old name, why should I have told you?" (เป็นชื่อเก่าทำไมนิมควรบอก...)

132. Ow: Expression of worry or concern (อ้าว)

133. Laew: Already (แล้ว)

134. Gahok: Liar (โกหก)

135. Bok wa...ta brien chua, ja me sombot neh non, ja hai chok dee kong chan nai chiwit neh non: "They said if I change my name I will be guaranteed fortune, it will guarantee luck in my life." (บอกว่าถ้าเปลี่ยนชื่อจะมีสมบัติแน่นอนก็เลยจะให้โชคดีของฉันในชีวิตแน่นอน)

136. Gai tod: Fried chicken (ไก่ทอด)

137. Krungthep: Bangkok (กรุงเทพ)

138. Phii: Ghosts (ผี)

139. Cha giew: Green tea (ชาเขียว)

140. Payanok: Serpent people (พญานาค)

141. Eyung wa: "What the hell?" (อิหยังวะ)

142. Nang sam phiu: "Three-skin lady." (นางสามผิว)

143. Lao Tay Arrom: "Whatever The Feeling Is" (แล้วแต่อารมณ์)

144. Ba-toh: Expression of surprise (ป๊าโธ่)

145. Nan dee: A phrase of agreement (นั่นดี)

146. Ti khou bok rou tang pai tom hai silajaruk: "...where they told us we had to go and summon a stone?" (ที่เขาบอกเราต้องไปทำศิลาจารึก)

147. Hai laew: "It's gone." (หายแล้ว)

148. yak kin moo ka tat yuu: "I want to eat some barbecue pork." (อยากกินหมูกระทะอยู่)

149. Tab lang: Votive stones for Lord Vishnu (ทับหลัง)

150. Prathet Thai: The country of Thailand (ประเทศไทย)

151. Kuy dai yen mai: "Have you heard?" (เคยได้ยินไหม)

152. Phra Narai: Lord Vishnu (พระนารายณ์)

153. Tab lang hai: "The stones disappeared." (ทับหลังหาย)

154. Mak: Very (มาก)

155. Aow Phra Narai kun ma: "Bring back Lord Vishnu." (เอาพระนารายณ์คืนมา)

156. Chang: Elephant (ช้าง)

157. Mai dai aow ma, krub, ga luy mai sai luy: "Never brought it, never wore it." (ไม่ได้เอามาครับก็เลยไม่ใส่เลย)

158. Wats: Temples (วัด)

159. Khob khun: "Thank you." (ขอบคุณ)

160. Talok: Funny (ตลก)

161. Pai nai: "Where are you going?" (ไปไหน)

162. Pai Wat Luang Ratcha: "I'm going to Wat Luang Ratcha." (ไปวัดหลวงราช)

163. Jing lor: "Really?" (จริงเหรอ)

164. Na ti dek: "A Child's Duty" (หน้าที่เด็ก)

165. Mong: Maybe (มั้ง)

166. Tom dai luy krub: "We can do this." (ทำได้เลยครับ)

167. Beb: "Like…" (แบบ)

168. Sombat chat tang rak sa: "National treasures must be preserved!" (สมบัติชาติต้องรักษา)

CPSIA information can be obtained
at www.ICGtesting.com
Printed in the USA
BVHW040705141222
654205BV00002B/27